Diana Pullein-Thompson left school at fourteen and for fifteen years taught riding, broke-in and schooled horses, and competed in many events. She also rode her part-bred Arab mare from John O'Groats to Land's End. She wrote her first book with her sisters at the age of fifteen and has now written thirty one books for children and several for adults. She is married to art historian, Dennis Farr, and lives in Surrey with her collie, Cleo.

THE LONG RIDE HOME

Diana Pullein-Thompson

CAVALIER PAPERBACKS

Published by Cavalier Paperbacks 1996

Burnham House
Jarvis Street
Upavon
Pewsey
Wilts SN9 6DU

ISBN 1-899470-21-2

Typeset in Century Schoolbook

Printed and bound by Cox and Wyman, Reading, Berks

AUTHOR'S NOTE

All the places in this story are imaginary.
Carey's journey bears no relation to my
own ride from John O'Groats to Land's End
in 1956, on my grey mare, Favorita, except
for the heart-warming and generous Scottish hospitality we both received from total
strangers.

CHAPTER ONE

I rode Sandpiper down to the ferry to meet my half-sister Hannah, while Mum walked beside me, her dark mane of hair tossed by the wind, her cheeks brightened by the sharp sea air.

I was very excited, because I had always longed for a sister, but I had never met Hannah, who was ten years older than me, because she had been brought up mainly in Australia. Would she have an Australian accent, I wondered, and resemble the characters in *Neighbours*, which in those days was one of my favourite television programmes? Had she been warned that our cottage on the island was a back to nature place with no electricity, telephone or running hot water? An escape for my parents, who were television personalities much troubled by fans, journalists and the trappings of modern life.

"She knows we only have the basics, doesn't she?" I asked Mum anxiously.

"Your father's told her everything," Mum said and frowned because Hannah had messed up carefully laid plans by coming a day later than arranged, which meant my mother could only shake her by the hand before catching the ferry back to the mainland herself. "Don't forget to give her the envelope on the kitchen table with all the instructions in it, so that she knows what to do in an emergency."

"You mean I might be one?" I asked, because my disability had put me permanently on the defensive.

"A what?"

"An emergency."

"Of course not, but at least, as a nurse, she should know how to manage your pills."

We arrived at the little harbour as the ferry came towards us dividing the waves in a great vee. "What does she look like?"

"Blonde, your father says, but don't forget he hasn't seen her for twenty years. Anyhow, the main thing is she has wonderful references from her hospital sister and she's talked on the phone for hours on end with your father, and they got on like houses on fire. But remember she's been brought up to hate me and that's why I wanted us to meet first, so that she could change her mind."

"Then she might hate me, too," I suggested.

"No, she's dying to meet you," Mum insisted, "and she says she doesn't believe everything her mother tells her."

Now as the passengers started to disembark, Mum held up a placard like travel couriers do at airports, which said in large black letters HANNAH LOVEGROVE, and suddenly my half-sister, dwarfed by a huge backpack, walked towards us with a broad smile on a face, half hidden by a big woolly cap and a scarf.

"My step-mother Melanie?" she asked. "I've seen you on television, so I know your face."

"Welcome to the island," Mum said, kissing her on both cheeks, "and this is your sister, Carey."

"I like the pony," Hannah said.

"Want to ride some of the way home," I asked.

"My backpack..." she grimaced.

"I could carry it," I said.

"No, it's too heavy for you, thanks all the same."

"There won't be a lot to do here," I warned, forgetting Mum. "I'm the only rider, but if you like wildlife..." My voice petered out, as I saw Hannah looking at a gaunt, red-bearded man.

"You've brought a friend with you?" asked Mum, who doesn't miss much."

"No, just someone I got talking to on the boat. He knows the bloke at the Wildlife Centre," Hannah said.

"Oh great!" cried Mum. "So you'll have a friend here."

"Maybe," Hannah said.

Now the passengers for the other islands or the return journey were beginning to embark and Mum hugged me.

"Darling we shall miss you so much. Now don't forget, go to the Centre if Hannah gets ill or something.

"Don't worry, Mrs Lovegrove, I'm never ill," Hannah said.

"There's always a first time," declared Mum with tears in her eyes. "See Carey takes her pills Hannah, and don't let her fall off. My mother - her name and telephone number are in the envelope - has our addresses if anything goes wrong, and Cosmo has your mobile phone number, so we can ring from time to time, can't we? And listen, Carey, call Granny, if something really awful happens and you need help. Take care darling." She kissed me and then ran up the gang plank, a tall, lithe figure, watched admiringly by those who knew her from her television chat show. I waved and waved until the ferry was a dot at sea, and then I said, "This way Hannah," and turned Sandpiper's head for home. And as we walked down the track across the moor, which leads to the cottage, the great golden eagles for which our island is famous, flew overhead.

"Brilliant!" cried Hannah. "I've wanted so much to see them."

"You knew they were here?"

"Oh yes, and the bloke I met on the boat filled me in."

"I hate it when they carry lambs in their talons."

"All part of the biological chain," said Hannah. "How old is your pony?"

"Six, he comes from another much larger island called Mull," I told her, "but we only holiday here in the summer, so he never gets enough exercise, such a waste. Would you like to try him tomorrow?"

"Maybe," Hannah said. "But first I must get used to being here. It's warmer than I expected."

As we neared the cottage we heard my dog, Tina, barking.

"She's a collie, and a brilliant guard," I explained.

"And this is her holiday too."

"In Australia dogs live outdoors," Hannah told me. "Are you sure she's not bad for your illness?"

"It's not really an illness," I replied reluctantly. "And Tina's my greatest friend." I stood up in my stirrups. "Look there's the cottage, see, Hannah?"

"Smaller than I expected. My father said it had three bedrooms. Is that right?"

"Absolutely," I said. And soon we were there, and I hitched Sandpiper up to a ring Dad had put in the wall and opened the front door. Tina came running and then stopped and raised her hackles at the sight and smell of Hannah.

"Tina, Tina, it's all right, Hannah's staying with us." I knelt down and put my arms round my dog. "Don't worry."

"You speak to her like a child."

"Is that a crime?" I asked suddenly nettled.

"Don't over-react. she's only a dog," Hannah said.

"I'll light the primus, would you like tea or coffee? There are scones, too," I said, knowing that hunger makes some people irritable.

"Primuses are dangerous," Hannah told me. "No calor gas?"

"No."

"But that's crazy."

"There's a wood burning stove, I can light if you like, but first I must take Sandpiper to his field, otherwise he'll pull back and break his reins."

"All right," Hannah said, and so the holiday, which was to become a nightmare, began.

11

CHAPTER TWO

When Hannah took off her scarf and woolly hat I saw that her hair ran down her back in one long fair plait. Her hooded eyes were pebble-blue and her nose sharp and rather elegant. She was shorter than me, shorter than I expected for my Dad, Cosmo, is very tall, and she had wide shoulders.

Busying myself with the primus, I told her we had an old fashioned range, too, that burnt coal delivered to us once a year. "That's what we use when we make bread or stews," I explained. "But we don't keep it on all the time, because, although there's always a wind from the sea, this place can get quite warm in summer."

"Where do you keep the coal?" Hannah asked.

"Out there in the shed. We've got three sheds, actually. Mum and Dad's bikes live in one."

"And what's in that?" she pointed to an oak chest Granny gave to my parents.

"I don't know."

"It has a key?" asked Hannah.

"Yes, do you want to look? I'm sure there's nothing

private inside."

I took the key off the chimney piece and opened the chest, which wasn't locked.

"Just a few climbing boots, a waste of space," Hannah said, peering inside."Now I must open this envelope."

She pulled out of it a wedge of five and ten pound notes and also several fifty pound ones.

"Good, my wages," she said. "One hundred pounds a week, not so much from a father who's never paid maintenance."

"And the housekeeping money is there too," I said. "We have to go to the mainland to buy all but the basics."

Hannah started to read my mother's letter.

"So you have fits," she said, frowning. "That is serious. Are you sure you should ride?"

I turned cold. "Not fits," I said, "black-outs, Hannah. I was terribly ill you see after I went with my parents to India. I had meningitis, terrible headaches and sickness. I went into a coma. Everyone, even the doctors, thought I was going to die, but I didn't, no, I hung on." My voice rose, as I remembered those awful weeks in hospital. "I was delirious."

"High temperatures cause fits," Hannah said, calm as stagnant water.

"No, not fits," I shouted, and hated myself for shouting. "Anyway, I'm all right now, so long as I take a pill twice a day."

"No one with fits is ever all right," Hannah said.

"Mum said that being a nurse you would remember my pills."

13

"And deal with a fit," Hannah insisted. "You poor girl!" As I started to make instant coffee I said, "I, of all people, should know what's wrong with me. The specialist said ..."

"Your mother says here," continued Hannah.

"Give it to me." I tried to grab the letter.

"No Carey, it's private."

"Mum doesn't hide things from me." I banged a mug down in front of Hannah.

"It is not always wise to tell patients everything," countered Hannah. "And you, Carey, are a very highly-strung girl."

Then Tina came, collie-like, and sat beside me, pressing her warm body against my legs and, to change the subject, I told Hannah that my parents planned a trip across all those countries which had recently broken away from the Soviet Union. "I expect Dad told you," I said, "They're writing a joint travel book. They've acted, presented TV shows, interviewed lots of famous people, and now they long to be published. The book's a new challenge. Would you like some oatcakes and honey?"

Hannah shook her head. "No calor gas. I don't believe it."

"Mum and Dad are very impractical," I said, stroking Tina's black and white fur. "In London they eat far too much in restaurants, so here it's all health food." I opened the cupboard, "See?" I pointed to cartons of fruit and vegetable juices, a yoghurt making machine, pots of honey stacked high. "The garden is full of peas and beans, carrots and new potatoes. Old

14

Mungo plants it out for us every spring, and we go down to the harbour and buy fish and cook some of it on long, toasting forks over the wood fire. It's great. Mungo's wife makes bread for us and Sandpiper lives in Mungo's field. He's a crofter. I'm so glad you're small. I thought you might be tall like Dad."

"My Ma's small," Hannah said.

"Which means you can share Sandpiper with me; we can take it in turns to ride as we explore the island. I've got a brilliant book on riding, so we can give each other dressage and jumping lessons in Mungo's field. Ever since Dad told me you liked riding I've been dreaming of this, honestly. Being the only child here is boring."

"I'm twenty three, adult," Hannah retorted, bursting in four snubbing words my balloon of hope.

"Yes of course, and you probably wouldn't like to be taught by me, even if I was keeping to the letter of the book."

"I don't like riding. Full stop," Hannah said.

"But Dad told me..."

"He lied to keep you happy. He's like that," Hannah remarked. "Grown-ups don't like kids kicking up a fuss."

"I'm not a kid."

"Teenagers then."

"He said you had ridden in the Bush."

"He invented that. Writers always invent, you know that."

"Dad doesn't lie."

"I don't think you know our father very well,"

Hannah said.

"I'm going out," I shouted.

"Who's going to light that hideous old range then?"

"We'll have sandwiches for lunch," I told her, before running from the house with Tina at my heels.

I went to Mungo's field and sat in the sparse grass and, looking out to sea, saw in the tranquil blue bay a yacht with its white sails folded, and above me once again a golden eagle, this time with a mouse in its talons. I heard the cry of the pee-wits and the distant bleating of sheep on the other side of the island and the more raucous sound of the sea gulls and, then I thought I saw, but I may have been mistaken, the sweet heads of two seals bobbing merrily in the waves. And I knew, in my heart of hearts, that Hannah, despite our shared father, would not appreciate all that the island offered. And I felt very lonely, until Sandpiper came and nuzzled in my pockets where sometimes I keep the green tops of carrots, which he loves.

I thought of my black-outs. Were they really fits, as Hannah said? Or was she trying to diminish me? Was she crazy with jealousy because Dad had left her mother for mine, and I was growing up with him, while she had been forced to come to terms with an Australian step-father she didn't like. Was she determined to punish me for something which wasn't my fault? I was angry then with my parents for leaving me with a girl they hardly knew. I remembered Granny accusing Mum of selfishness. "You've got to take responsibility for your own daughter," she had shouted. "Not drag her round the world with you, like a bag of potatoes, exposing her to every germ there is. Child first, career second."

After meningitis I had spent six months living with Granny in her cottage on the edge of the Yorkshire moors. As I grew stronger, Mum had paid for me to have riding lessons there at the local school and I took Tina for long walks across heather clad hills. Sometimes, when work allowed, one or both my parents stayed at an inn close by to be with me. They came loaded with presents, as though they were trying to make up for leaving me with Granny, but I soon thought of that little, old Yorkshire cottage as home, and when the time came I didn't want to go back to London with Mum and Dad, or worse still, to my convent boarding school with all its rules and regulations. Now suddenly sitting in this Scottish field, with Sandpiper digging in my pockets and Tina at my side, I longed to tell Granny about Hannah, to ask her advice and, perhaps, giggle with her a little about Hannah's behaviour. I decided then that I would wait a couple of days and if matters didn't improve I would go to the Wildlife Centre and borrow their phone and consult the person I trusted more than anyone else in the world on what I should do.

CHAPTER THREE

Next morning, after finishing her third mug of instant coffee, Hannah handed me my first tablet of the day.

"Are you really allowed to ride alone?" she asked as I swallowed it.

"Of course."

"You father and Melanie don't want to admit your disease is serious, do they?"

"It isn't; it's caused by a very minor fault in the electrical mechanism of the brain, that's all. I think I'm lucky to be alive," I said, "and now I'm off."

"Where to?"

"To see Sandpiper."

"You have warnings of these attacks?"

"I don't have attacks and my black-outs are in the past. Please may we drop the subject?"

"I'm here to look after you, so I must know the facts."

"Now you have them." I ran from the room, followed by Tina. I fetched Sandpiper's saddle, bridle and grooming kit from the nearest shed and hurried down the track that leads to his field. Sandpiper was standing head to tail with Mungo's grey garron mare,

Morag, but whinnied sweetly when he saw me. I fed him a few pony nuts from my pockets, and then I groomed him, tacked up and we were off.

As we passed the cottage Hannah came running out. "At least tell me where you're going," she said.

"Down by the ferry," I replied, "and a long way round to a little cove, which lies beyond the cottages which once belonged to fishermen, and up over the hill."

Hannah screwed up her face. "I saw a weirdo on that path," she said.

"You've been exploring already?" I wanted to add angrily "without me", for Hannah seemed bent on destroying every figment of my perfect sister dream, but I didn't, because I thought we had already exchanged too many cross words.

"You bet!" she said. "I don't let the grass grow under my feet."

"Probably someone on his way to the Wildlife Sanctuary," I suggested. "Bird watchers often look rather weird. See you!"

I squeezed Sandpiper with my calves, opened my fingers on the reins and he trotted away down the track, head high, ears pricked, joy in every stride.

Everywhere on the island, which is wild with two mountains humped like a camel's back, you can hear the roar of the sea and the gulls calling. You can smell the heather, myrtle, peat and pine, a mixture lovelier than the loveliest bowl of pot pourri. And the ever changing sky is wide and low, often with such glorious sunsets and delicate unforgettable dawns, that you forget the grey days when the rain sweeps across the landscape and the clouds are low. I love the dark rocks, too, and the empty white beaches and the great stretches of moor where the pee-wits cry and the gaunt black faced sheep which spring so easily over every ditch or fence in their way. After school, after London, the island intoxicates me, while its very beauty increases my loneliness. Riding or walking, I escape into fantasy. Playing in my mind with words, I sometimes become a poet or a famous author or even, in moments of greater imagination, a pop singer. Pop is forbidden at my boarding school. My parents hate it, too. But in a drawer in my bedroom in our London flat is a well hidden picture of my favourite star, dark, black eyed Lucian Manelli. I take it out sometimes and gaze at his lean, tormented face and think if only we could meet!

Now, with my mind so far away, I soon found myself at the shore. It was low tide, I reined-in Sandpiper, so that I could look more closely at the yacht. Why was it there? Hank Wassenberg, the American millionaire, from whom my parents leased the cottage, had surely not come back. Now I saw, also, a dinghy moored by the rocks with a seagull balancing on its bows. Tina, who notices every change on our side of the island, which she considers to be her territory, ran down to inspect the alien boat and returned with a plastic packet in her mouth.

"Drop, drop! I dismounted and she spat out a packet of peanuts, saliva-wet outside, but dry within. As I examined this, she sat watching, her eyes searching mine, a little spittle forming at the corners of her mouth.

"Oh all right," I said, "We'll share them," and instantly, as though understanding my words, Sandpiper pushed forward for his share, stepping on my toes.

Afterwards stuffing the empty packet in my pocket, I wondered guiltily whether we had eaten somebody's emergency rations, for on an island where almost everything comes by sea, all food is treasured and a week of bad weather can leave the improvident hungry.

I dismounted to rest Sandpiper, as we climbed the steep path towards the Wildlife Centre, but we turned back before reaching its gates taking the wider track that leads you down again, from which, on a clear day, you can look across the sea to the mainland and the gentle green hills beyond the harbour there. Cars and vans with four-wheel drives are sometimes allowed to go along that way from the ferry terminal, vehicles much hated by my parents who came to the island to escape from traffic and the stink of petrol and oil.

"If only we could import some mules," Dad once said.

Back at the cottage, I tied Sandpiper to the ring on the wall and went inside. Lunch, I thought, Mungo's eggs scrambled on the primus and peas and potatoes from the garden. (I wanted to cook, so that this half-sister of mine would have to rely on me in at least one respect). Then, meeting spirals of cigarette smoke and the babble of several voices, I stopped dead. Tina barked wildly at the four people sitting round the living room table. Strange people, all different.

"Oh here's Carey." Hannah turned her head but remained seated. "Meet my friends." She waved an arm as though to embrace them all. "Friends from afar you could say." The bearded man she spoke to at the Ferry terminal, called, "Hi Carey, pleased to meet you. I'm Steve."

"Hi!" My voice was low-key, while I tried to absorb the situation. "Quite a party," I added.

"Join us," suggested Steve, "Have a fag? This, by the way, is Mercy." He touched a small, dark girl on the shoulder, "from the Philippines."

"An au-pair," said Hannah.

Mercy got to her feet, and, as she kissed me on the cheek, even I could tell, from mixing with my parents' friends, that the scent she wore was too expensive to be bought from an au-pair's wages. But maybe, I thought, she has a wealthy boyfriend.

"I hope you enjoy your stay on the island," I said.

"So old fashioned," cried Steve, "Relax, Carey."

"It's a convent upbringing," I explained. "Holy sisters insist on manners at all times."

"You're lovely." Mercy spoke in an accent I could not identify. "A typical English girl."

"Did you come in the yacht?" I asked.

"What yacht?" grinned Steve. "I came by ferry. You saw me."

"A Yacht, is there a yacht?" asked Mercy, her voice striking a false note.

"You can't miss it," I said.

The second man hadn't spoken, small and dark he was just a little like my brilliant Lucian. Did he know any English? I was too shy to ask. The coolness of the visitors, except for Steve, made me feel terribly young and foolish. I was in a muddle, an outsider in the midst of strangers.

Now Hannah cleared her throat. "Listen folks," she began importantly "Our young friend Carey, suffers from a distressing illness, so if anyone sees her lying on the floor, kicking and twisting, fetch me at once. I'm here to look after her."

"No," I shouted, sure that she was trying to belittle me in the others' eyes. My disability is private, my own affair and it's cured, sorted out." And because shouting was a crime at school I felt guilty, as well as angry and added, "Sorry," as an afterthought.

"Poor Carey," crooned Mercy. "I understand. We invade your house and then talk about your personal problems. It's not right. We'll stop it, do you others hear me?"

"Want a cold hamburger?" asked Steve, watching me slyly from the corners of his deep brown eyes.

"No, no thanks. I must take Sandpiper to his field or he'll pull back and break his reins."

As Tina and I made for the door, Hannah said, "Carey's standard get-away excuse."

"No, no" argued Mercy. "We should all be kind to her. Do not forget this girl is without mother or father, only the dog to love, amid the fits, those terrible fits. We should pity her. She's a cripple."

Walking to the field leading Sandpiper, I was furious with my parents for not telling me so many people were coming to the cottage, and furious with myself for being selfish enough to hate them for being there. Dad must have known if he talked to Hannah for hours on end, as Mum said.

Yet he let me suppose only Hannah and I would be there. Perhaps after all, I thought, Hannah is right and he tells me half-truths. Perhaps I do have fits, my black-outs; perhaps I make a fool of myself writhing and kicking on the ground, or worse. Probably everyone on the island knows about the fits, and pities me, because of that time I blacked-out on the shore as the ferry came in, before the medical specialist sorted me out. Perhaps even old Mungo says pityingly to tourists, "There goes the bonnie English lassie who has the fits."

I sat in the field for a long time with Tina, feeling sorry for myself before, at last, I picked myself up and made my way reluctantly back to the cottage.

CHAPTER FOUR

"In my country," Mercy said, "the people eat dogs. Sometimes they take their pets for a picnic and then suddenly kill and roast them on a fire."

"You're winding me up," I said.

"It's true," Steve insisted.

"You're joking! Have you been to the Philippines?" I asked.

"Just once."

"And you?" I look at the dark haired silent man, not wanting him to feel left out, and nodding, he held up one stumpy finger.

"Franco understands English but can't speak it," Hannah explained.

Tina growled, then got up and paced the room. And I realised she was now growling whenever my half-sister spoke, and that worried me, because some dogs sense evil before humans do.

"That collie should be outside. She's a farm animal," Hannah said, "Not a pet. She smells and brings in mud."

"Haven't you heard of mudpacks, which people put

on their faces?" I asked. "Mud is clean and Tina smells of heather and Scottish earth and anyway this cottage is her home." I wanted to add "not yours", but thought that might be too rude. After all, somehow we had got to live together for five weeks.

We were sitting round the table eating soup, followed by bread and cheese and fruit when Steve and Mercy changed their tone and tried to be nice to me. They asked me politely about my school and my grandmother.

"Which reminds me I must phone Granny," I said.

"What for?" asked Hannah.

"Just for a chat. Sometimes she gets lonely. Can I borrow your mobile?"

"I forgot to bring it." Hannah said, without emotion.

"You're joking!"

"It's true."

"But you promised Dad."

"Tough luck!"

And you told Mum you had one and she said she would ring us on your number, the number you gave to Dad, don't you remember?"

"When I unpacked, it wasn't there, just one of those things," Hannah said.

"Her memory is pathetic," added Steve.

"All right, we all make mistakes," I said. "Give me some money and I'll go to the mainland and buy another. Then we can tell Granny and she'll tell Mum when Mum rings her," I said.

"Quick thinking," exclaimed Steve, "But mobile phones don't come cheap. In London you might pick

26

one up for thirty quid. But up here in the wilds ..."

"Mum's left Hannah with lots of money," I pointed out.

"I'm not squandering that on a phone," Hannah said.

"Then you must write and ask for your phone to be posted on," I insisted. "Please Hannah."

"I don't know where I left the wretched thing," cried Hannah, before shouting, as Tina growled, "Kick that dog out Steve!"

"You dare!" I cried, and Tina came and pressed herself against my legs.

"Wind down," said Steve, staring hard at Hannah. "Both of you."

"None of you want a phone, do you?" I shouted, "You actually want us to be marooned here."

Steve got up. "I think it's time for a wee dram of whisky, don't you? Before nerves get frayed." He went to my parents' drinks' cupboard for a bottle and glasses. "Carey?"

"I'm not allowed to drink until I'm eighteen," I said.

"Good girl!" exclaimed Hannah, with a hint of mockery in her voice. "Anyhow, it wouldn't mix with the drugs you're taking."

"I'm not taking drugs."

"All medicines are drugs," declared Hannah. "Bed for you, I think, Carey, it's been a long day."

"Yeah, past nine," Steve said.

And I knew they wanted me to go so that they could get down to business. But what business? That was the vital question and how was I to find the answer?

Then I asked to speak to Hannah alone and she said,

27

"Whatever for?" and I said, "It won't take a moment."

We went into the damp little scullery, where Tina edged Hannah into a corner.

"What's the big deal?" Hannah asked.

"You haven't given me my evening pill," I said. "And please let me have the bottle, because I'm fourteen now and I can handle it. And, by the way, my problem is private. I don't want your friends talking about it."

"No," Hannah set her jaw. "I shall stick by the promise I made to our father."

"But you don't mind breaking your promise about the phone," I said. "Mum will be so worried when she finds she can't get through."

"Tough," said Hannah again. "Come on, let's get back to the others."

And then I wanted to say: You really don't care, do you, because you hate me, because Dad left you and your mother for my Mum, and it's not my fault, is it? but the words wouldn't come.

"I'll fetch your tablet," Hannah said, as though she was granting me a great favour, "Just trust me, Carey."

Then as she moved towards the living room, Tina grabbed her ankle and bit it and the blood ran down her red socks into her Doc Marten shoes.

"Bad, bad Tina," I cried, half pleased and half sorry. "I'm sorry Hannah, it's the first time she has ever bitten anybody."

"I bet! I'll kill her one of these days! Steve, I've been bitten."

28

Her friends came running - or were they, I thought wildly, her accomplices? - and Steve looked at me and said "the first aid kit, Carey."

I fetched it from the bathroom and then I went up to my room with Tina and, I'm sorry to say, I cried. I cried because Mum and Dad were far away and I couldn't speak to them and because the cottage had been invaded by people I didn't know and didn't like. Most of all, I cried because Hannah had said my black-outs were fits and she held the tablets which kept me well - if only, I thought she had come before my meningitis, I would not be in her power. Finally I cried out of self pity, because my dream of the perfect sister had been demolished.

Then I realised, of course, that Hannah had still not given me my evening pill, and I would have to plead for it, and I couldn't wash my tear-stained face first, because in our cottage you have to pass through the living room to reach a cold tap. Creeping downstairs, my heart like lead, I heard Hannah say, in a voice which seemed English rather than Australian, "Don't worry, I'll see Carey doesn't cause any problems."

In a haze of cigarette smoke she and her friends were leaning over a map, which they quickly folded up when I appeared.

"What do you want?" Hannah's harshness made my heart beat faster.

"My tablet."

"Oh yes! That vicious dog drove it right out of my mind. If she bites anyone else she will have to be put down, you know that, don't you?"

She dug the bottle of tablets out of her shoulder bag and gave me one.

"There's no hot water, I suppose," Steve said.

"Only if you heat it on the primus or light the range - see, the range has a tap; you carry the water from there to the bath. Mum once stayed in an old Spanish villa with that arrangement, only they burned charcoal, not coal."

"How crazy can you be?" cried Steve. "Why no proper boiler for Pete's sake? Your Mum and Dad can't be short of cash."

"Don't ask me," I said, for it was a question I had often turned over in my own mind. "Perhaps they're acting out the past."

"Media people and their fantasies - they are all nuts," Hannah said. "Now go to bed, Carey - I can see you've been crying - and get some sleep. You look dreadful. And tomorrow that dog is to be locked in a shed. Right?"

"Only when you're around," I said.

I lay awake a long time, listening to the strangers' voices murmuring in the living room. What brought them here? Steve was obviously Hannah's friend and tonight they would sleep together in my parents' bed, but what about the others? And why should Mercy want to come to a remote Scottish island? A girl from a hot climate, who showed no interest in wildlife. And the Lucian look-alike?

Now it was a clear night, light as day, for darkness comes late in Scotland's summers, but instead of being happy, as I had once hoped, I was lonelier than at any other time in my life. An outsider in my own home, managed by someone I was beginning to hate. Mum had left me fifteen pounds, which was not enough to buy a phone. There was an English family in the big house on the far side of the island, but they didn't like us, largely because Dad had kicked up a fuss when they turned an old lady out of her cottage. So, as Mum said, there was only the Wildlife Centre, which we understood had a fax machine as well as a phone. From there early next morning I would ring Granny and she would tell me what to do. My mind made up at last, I slept.

Then suddenly I was wide awake; someone was standing at my side with fair hair tumbling over her shoulders - Hannah. Tina barked.

"Get hold of that dog. If she bites me again I'll take your parents to court. Right!"

"What's happened?" I said, as I grabbed Tina's collar. My first thought was for my parents. Had they met with an accident on their perilous journey across the Caucasus?

"You've had a fit, Carey. I'm going to give you a tablet."

"I haven't. I'm fine," I said.

"People have them at night and don't know anything about it next morning. I heard you, Carey, thrashing about."

"I'm only allowed two tablets every twenty four hours, whatever happens, so that's it," I said.

"This is a different sort to help you sleep, so tomorrow you'll feel fine. I'm a nurse. I know, and our Dad said I must use my medical experience to keep you well. Come on now, be a sensible girl. Otherwise I'll forbid you to ride Sandpiper. There's no way out. You're under my control, Carey."

She held the tablet in one hand. "Open your mouth and I'll pop it in."

"It could be poison."

"Oh, Carey, are you mad? What a terrible thing to say. Look, see, here is the name on the tablet, see, Mogadon, does that sound like poison?"

Somewhere in the back of my brain that name rang a bell. Mum talking, Mum saying a friend had taken a Mogadon to help her sleep, and I felt a fool - over-reacting again.

"It's a sleeping pill."

"Right, clever girl. And it will help you recover from your little attack, because you do feel awful, don't you?"

And I heard my voice whisper "Yes," as though I was being pressed by a nun into making a confession, for I was totally drained by worry and confusion. It was, also, the middle of the night when resistance is low and it's hard to be strong if you are wakened suddenly from a deep and dream-ridden sleep. So I swallowed the pill and then drank from the glass of water Hannah offered me, while I held Tina with my other hand, and I heard my voice say, "Thank you," still in that ghostly whisper.

"Good girl," said Hannah, before leaving the room and shutting the door gently behind her.

CHAPTER FIVE

Tina wakened me by nudging my face and whining.
The cottage was very quiet; the clear skies of the night
had been replaced by low clouds and a thin drizzle of
soft rain. The roar of the sea was gentle; the birds
and gulls were silent. Where was everybody? My
watch said eleven o'clock. So the Mogadon had worked
all too well and I had been left to sleep on. I splashed
my face with cold water, pulled on jeans and a tee
shirt, lit the primus and made myself porridge, which
I ate with honey and milk. Then I opened a tin of dog
meat for Tina which I mixed with Winalot and hot
water. Half of me was pleased to be alone in the cottage and the other half was sorry - if only Hannah
had come up to my expectations! I went to the nearest shed and filled my pockets with pony nuts from a
sack there. Looking round I saw two empty crates.
Then, missing coffee, I collected my tack and ran to
Sandpiper's field. Ten minutes later I was riding along
the track which climbs gradually to the Wildlife Centre, which stands on the edge of cliffs, looking out to
sea.

Why did Dad tell me Hannah loved riding, dogs and wildlife. "She won't miss TV," he had added, "because she's reading all Jane Austen's books and, maybe, a bit of Proust, too. It's a real bonus to discover she's literary. Who knows - I might even find her a job over here, as a change from nursing."

"Who was lying?" I asked myself now. "Dad to convince Melanie and me that I should be happy? Or Hannah, because for some obscure reason she wanted to come to the island?" Revenge. The word seemed to come from nowhere, but when I'm in London I watch television for hours on end. I also read newspapers and from these two sources, so disliked by the nuns at school, I know that revenge can drive the most law-abiding people to violence. So was Hannah here to wreck in some way our lives, because she thought Dad had wrecked hers and her mother's?

Now looking back I saw two figures on the yacht and the little dinghy bobbing in its wake. Were the boats there as a quick getaway? Supposing Mum and Dad returned to find the cottage burned down and their daughter missing? Such a tragedy seemed possible, because earlier in the year I had read of a Moroccan student who had killed his girlfriend's parents and their pet - a Dutch Barge dog - in revenge for her leaving him.

Soon it stopped raining and all the earth, the trees and flowers shone. Sandpiper, who was unshod, picked his way carefully over rocks and boulders, and then at last we came close to the Centre, a long low wooden building, and we could hear the seabirds calling far below, and the song of the sea against the cliffs. Then I started to wonder what I would say: I'm in a fix. Mum and Dad are away, and I need to ring Granny. Please may I borrow your phone? or I'm sorry to bother you, but there's a bit of an emergency and I wonder whether you could let me use your phone. Nothing sounded right, because nothing does if you say it over and over again. Then a little breeze, soft as satin, touched my cheeks; the muted red of the pine trunks sharpened; the grass turned to emerald and Sandpiper's dun coat to the richest gold. And suddenly I was afraid, for I knew what this meant. I dismounted quickly, put out my hands to save my face and then the heather rose to meet me as I fell.

I came round to find grass in my mouth and Sandpiper grazing a few yards away. Tina licked my cheeks and one of the golden eagles flew overhead, its talons empty. I sat for a bit, collecting my wits. Then I stumbled to a burn, and for the second time that morning, splashed my face with cold water. Then leading Sandpiper, I went to the iron gates, which keep the unwanted out and rang the bell.

A young man with lots of thick black hair and a dark beard, came.

"Yes?" he said.

"I'm sorry to bother you, but I need to phone and ours has got left on the mainland. It's urgent."

"Oh you're the Lovegrove girl, aren't you, from the cottage next to old Mungo's croft?"

"Yes," I replied, "that's right. Mum said to come here."

"Well, I've got news for you." His grin showed perfect white teeth.

"Oh, has Mum phoned?"

"No your minder's here."

"My half-sister Hannah?"

"That's it - Hannah, an Aussie." He grinned again, as though enjoying a private joke. "Want to see her?"

"No, no thank you."

"She tells me she's over here to sort out your troubles, so I guess you need to ask her first."

"I've changed my mind," I told him, fighting back tears for I felt terribly weak.

Then I mounted and, feeling washed-out, started to ride home, only it wasn't home any more. And the naturalist's voice called after me, "Put that dog on the lead." But I didn't. Why should I when she was so perfectly trained?

Had anyone seen me lying on the ground? And did Hannah deliberately decide not to give me my tablet to prove her power against me? Those two questions ran through my head again and again, like the line of a song that is hateful yet haunts the mind.

Back in the cottage at last, I lit the primus and made myself coffee and ate oatcakes and honey and then noticed the key of the chest had gone, I tried to lift the lid, but it was locked. Then I looked in the sheds and found that one of the crates was sealed and too heavy to lift and next to it were Mum and Dad's boots. Moments later I heard Steve chatting in my parents' bedroom. To whom? I crept upstairs and through a crack in the door I saw him talking on a mobile phone.

"Yeah," he said, "we can deal with the girl. Sure she's neurotic, but that makes things easier. We can always dose her to the eyeballs. Yeah, of course we can, accidents do happen to girls in her condition. Yeah, everything's in hand. No worry. Right. Speak to you soon, ciao!"

Then, still befuddled by my black-out, I behaved like a fool and rushing in cried, "Why didn't you tell me you had a phone?"

"You were listening at the door," he said, slowly. "You dirty little creep."

"Not really - I heard voices and came up. Did you buy one on the mainland after all.

"It's none of your business."

"Sorry Steve, but please can I borrow it?"

"No, you must ask Hannah."

"Why?"

"Because she's in charge of you."

"She forgot my tablet. I could have fallen off a cliff and been killed. Is that what you want?"

You've got to behave herself," was all Steve said, and then I knew that this was the worst nightmare of my life, worse than the meningitis, because then my parents were there and the medics were fighting for me, whereas now I was totally alone. Yet in a strange way my illness had strengthened me, because it had taught me that it is possible to survive the most terrible experiences. And on that long summer evening I meant to survive this one, whatever happened.

CHAPTER SIX

I had decided to be cool, although deep inside I was
dead scared. So when Steve said, "Cook us supper,
will you, Carey, there's a good girl?" as he sat on the
sofa with his arm round Hannah. I said "right," and
forced a smile. I saw he had relaxed, since I told him
I had not heard a word of his telephone conversation.
"Just the murmur of your voice," I said.

My visit to the Wildlife Centre was not mentioned
by either of them. I didn't care. I had made a plan.

"Duncan McGregor's kippers, they came in with the
ferry?"

"Great, real Scottish grub," said Steve.

I went out into the garden and dug new potatoes,
and picked runner beans. I didn't want to light the
range, because it would make the living room too hot.
Instead I would cook the food in turn on the primus,
the vegetables first and then the kippers, whose salt
would add to my unwelcome guests' thirst.

"A drink?" I suggested on my return.

"Oh great!" said Steve.

"Help yourselves," I opened the cupboard door." Dad keeps a good store for when people come to stay."

"I fancy a gin and tonic," said Hannah.

They were both happy this evening, as though some terrible crisis had been overcome or some challenge met, to which I suspected the locked chest bore witness.

"Let's pretend it's a feast," I suggested. "Look, this is Dad's favourite claret - ten pounds a bottle - and there's a benedictine or cognac for afterwards."

"And vodka too," added Steve, standing behind me. "Let's get pissed on that."

"We can lie in tomorrow," Hannah added. "We were up at five this morning, while you, of course, were sleeping like a log. It's not surprising I forgot your tablet."

"You won't let me use Steve's phone I suppose. I want to give Granny the number just in case ...."

"They'll never get through from the Caucasus. The lines there are a nightmare. There's absolutely no point in bothering your poor old Granny," insisted Hannah.

"Oh all right, have it your own way," I smiled. I kept smiling all evening, because, miraculously, they were fitting in with all my plans, and I could hardly believe my good luck. I filled their glasses again.

After supper Hannah gave me my evening tablet - it was weird how those little white pills had begun to dominate my life - and I washed up while Steve and Hannah got drunk. When they had stopped giggling and bragging, and looked heavy-eyed, I suggested they went to bed and they did.

Then I boiled an egg, which I packed with the last of the bread and a hunk of Mrs Mungo's homemade cheese, in two little parcels, one for each pocket. Then I crept upstairs, to the sound of Steve and Hannah's snores. Their door was unlocked; they were sleeping fully dressed, back to back. It was twelve o'clock, but still light. I picked Hannah's shoulder bag off the floor, grabbed my bottle of tablets and took from her wallet two fifty pound notes, five ten and three five, telling myself I was merely retrieving the salary she had been wrongly paid for looking after me. I lay on my bed, but soon gave up trying to sleep and wishing I had a saddle bag, got up and gathered together the belongings I would need: a pen knife, spoon, tin opener, clean socks and pants, a jersey, comb, picnic plate and mug, toothpaste and brush - and rolled them up in my light-weight, waterproof sleeping bag which I tied with string, from a huge roll someone had given Dad as a joke one Christmas. I put a note saying, GONE TO STAY WITH MY AUNT AT FORT WILLIAM FOR A FEW DAYS - CAREY, on the kitchen table. At five o'clock, shaking with excitement, I made myself a bowl of porridge and fed Tina. Then I carried first the tack and a dandy brush to the field, and secondly the now sausage-shaped sleeping bag, which I eventually tied to the saddle's safety catches, as they seemed stronger than the Dees. Sandpiper, who was dozing in a corner, managed a squeaky sort of whinny before I gave him pony nuts from my pocket. He was groomed and tacked-up, before I remembered I needed a map, because since he was unused to heavy traffic, I would have to keep to smaller roads. I ran back to the cottage and straight into a yellow-faced Steve going to the bathroom.

"Up already?" he said. "My head! Some hangover."

"Best to sleep it off," I told him.

"So right," he muttered. "Poor mad Carey."

My parents had a shelf of maps, but their scale was so large that I would have needed several to guide me to Yorkshire, so I pocketed the one which covered the first fifty miles. Then I mounted Sandpiper and made for the early ferry, which I knew brought mail and newspapers at eight o'clock, some of which an old man, who lived in a fisherman's cottage, delivered on our side of the island. The rest were held in Mrs Murray's little shop for collection. In the past I had seen cattle and sheep on the ferry but no pony, except for Sandpiper, after my parents bought him in Mull.

This morning the sea was smooth; the lovely humped mountains shrouded in mist, while a pale sun cast a soft light over the tiny harbour. And I wondered where my parents were, tramping along wet pot-holed roads with their backpacks, or eating dumplings and beef in a restaurant, or caught up in the fighting which seemed to erupt so often in the countries which had once belonged to Russia?

At last the ferry came and I asked for tickets for Tina, Sandpiper and myself, but the ferry master said, "Och aye, but you should have warned me you were bringing the wee horse. We like a reservation you see."

"But you won't turn me away?"

And I felt the blood drain from my face as the ferry master looked me up and down with blue eyes sunk deep in a rugged face.

"You are off on your own then?" he asked.

"To stay with a friend, and get the pony shod," I replied.

"I ken you - the Lovegrove Lass, sixteen years old, I'm thinking," the ferry master said. "Your mother and father are media folk. Isn't that so? I like them very well. All right, all right, we'll find a space for the wee pony to be sure."

Smiling, I paid our fares, Sandpiper walked on to the ferry like a seasoned traveller, and our long ride home began.

CHAPTER SEVEN

"I see you have your sleeping bag and all," a ginger
haired man said, "Will ye be kipping down in the
heather then?"

"No, no, I'm going to relations," I stammered, suddenly almost too tired to think straight.

"Going hame to England then, to civilization you
might say?" he suggested.

"Fort William," I lied and I hated myself for lying,
because if you're educated in a convent you either go
against it and lie all the time or you always try to
speak the truth and, perhaps priggishly, I belonged
to the second group.

"I see you've got your collie as a guard."

"That's Tina," I said, moving to the other side of Sandpiper, who was being patted by a young girl, because
I disliked the man for his curiosity.

"What do you call his colour?" the girl asked.

"Dun with black points."

She took a bite from a cheese-filled bap before saying, " and what's his name? And, as I answered, Sandpiper seized the bap and ate it.

"Oh, the naughty wee horse," the girl's mother cried.

"He likes home cooking," a farmer said, and a small boy fed Sandpiper on peppermints, while I apologised for his thieving, while thinking ruefully that my flight had been witnessed by so many people that I had little hope of escape if the police came in search of me. Hannah and Steve would of course play on my disability if they reported my disappearance. They would suggest my black-outs were caused by mental instability, so that my suspicions would not be believed. Only Granny could help me, as she had helped me before after my terrifying attack of meningitis. I could see her now as the ferry cut through the blue white-crested waves, small and strong with a sharp nose and violet eyes, and a mouth, which was sometimes stern but more often smiling ironically at the many twists she saw in life. Granny would tell me exactly what to do because she was never at a loss for a word.

Presently the boat stopped briefly at another island to collect and deliver mail and passengers, before heading straight for the mainland. Then, straining my eyes, while Sandpiper yanked impatiently at his bit, I could just see the white cottages on the quayside, cottages, which never failed to raise a cheer from Dad, whose excitement at arriving anywhere was, Granny said, all part of his travel bug. The cottages came nearer and nearer and then we were there.

Sandpiper dragged me down the ramp, while Tina nipped at his heels yapping disgracefully.

Getting my land legs, I bought a bar of chocolate at the first shop I saw, so that I'd have change for a call, and then dithered outside a telephone kiosk, wondering how I could explain why I had brought Sandpiper with me. "Couldn't you have left him in Mungo's field," Granny would ask. "That's his home, isn't it?" And what would I say? Sitting on a bench, searching for an answer, I wondered whether I had read and seen so many horror and detective stories that, in my overheated imagination, I thought my pony might be taken hostage? But no, it wasn't this; in my heart of hearts, I knew the truth was that I had always hated him being so far away and Yorkshire was at least nearer to London than the island. I knew too, that Hannah, Steve and their friends had somehow destroyed for me the magic of my parents' hideaway. I would never feel the same again about it.

The matter settled, I went to the kiosk, inserted the right coins and dialled Granny's number and was half-glad when there was no reply. All right, I would leave this town and ride on. I knew the way South, down small, winding roads with passing places, to a loch, where I had twice picnicked with my parents. Here I shared my first cheese sandwich and one boiled egg with Tina, and Sandpiper grazed the sparse, salt-whipped grass. We all drank from a brown burn, before I consulted the map. The way looked easy. If the weather stayed fine I would sleep under the stars. If rain came I would find a bed and breakfast place and tell the owners I was seventeen. But first I would take the back roads to a smaller town where I could stock-up with provisions and buy meat and biscuits for Tina. Suddenly, for the first time since Mum left I felt really happy, because at last I was in charge of myself.

The smaller town had several shops, a castle, post office and stationers, and two hotels. I put Sandpiper's headcollar which he had carried round his neck, over his bridle and tied its rope to a ring, meant for dogs, outside a small supermarket. I told Tina to "Sit, stay," and went inside. I bought a one pound bag of complete dog food, which had to be mixed with water, two tins of pets' meat, a packet of spillers' shapes, porridge oats, a loaf of bread, cheese and two apples, which the check-out girl packed in a carrier bag for me. While I untied Sandpiper he put his nose into the bag and whipped out the loaf, eating half of it before I could stop him and covering the rest with green saliva.

"Oh no, you you..." I began, but what could I say? He had carried me seven or eight miles and was hungry. We found a grassy knoll beyond the town, where Tina and I sat for ten minutes while he grazed. Then I fed him a pile of oats and gave Tina a tin of meat with the rest of the bread mixed in, and ate two apples myself. The stream close by was dirty with plastic bottles, so I went to a terraced cottage and asked the aproned woman, who came to the door, whether she could spare a little water for us all. And she said, "Lord, yes, just be waiting a minute," and brought a bucketful for Tina and Sandpiper, which they barely touched and a cup of tea and a scone for me. She asked me where I was going and when I told her the next village, she said she had a sister there, right by the kirk, so if I needed help just knock on the door.

Riding on, I thought if everyone was so kind, I would definitely continue all the way to Granny's, a dream which was taking root in my mind like an acorn in the ground. Surely this would prove to everyone that my disability didn't matter, because I could handle it perfectly well by myself, thank you very much. My parents would be pleased, after all, because they like stamina and what they call grit.

And next time I saw my medical specialist I would mention what I had done, and he would smile and pat me on the back and say, "Congratulations!" And I would tell the Hungarian boy who lived in the flat above ours in London, and Emma, my best friend at school, and Kirsty the girl I met at the riding school near Granny's place. Then for a while I would be a female hero, and my fits, if they were fits, would be totally forgotten.

CHAPTER EIGHT

Riding mainly through sheep country with stretches
of moorland, heather-clad hills, dotted with stunted
rowans, and a few fenced fields, I saw it would not be
easy to sleep in the open. Tina would stay with me,
but Sandpiper might wander off and then I might
waste a whole day looking for him. So, when evening
came and hunger gnawed at my stomach and the bag
of food weighed heavy on my left arm, I asked for a
night's board at a low white-washed inn.

Tall, pine-thin and balding on top, the English landlord looked me over as though I was a pony for sale.

"Not under sixteen, are you?" he hazarded.

"Of course not. Do you think my Mum would let me
out alone if I was?" I managed a grin.

He sighed.

"I can't sell you any alcohol," he said. "I don't say
you're lying, but I've been caught out before. The
sooner identity cards come in the better, as far as I'm
concerned."

"I'm happy with Scottish water," I said. "I'm heading south so will leave early."

"Duke of Edinburgh Award, is it? " he asked, giving me a loophole I would not have thought of myself.

"That's right,"I said, thinking, *white lies, Carey, in a good cause*.

"In my mother's day, bless her, girls went out to work at fourteen, and do you know George the Third's grandson fought in the Peninsular War when he was that age?"

"No, that's news to me," I said, guessing this landlord didn't have enough people to talk to. "Do you by any chance, have a field or stable for my pony?"

"You're in luck," he replied, eying me quizzically with brown eyes under bushy brows set high in a lean craggy face. "The character I bought this place from had a donkey and cart - funny old chap, brown as a berry and wrinkled as a crab apple that's been left too long on the tree - and, bless him, he left me a bit of hay and straw."

"Brilliant," I said.

"This way." As the landlord took me to the small, broken-down stable, he told me his grandmother had married at seventeen and emigrated to South Africa, where she managed five native servants and had ten children. How's that for courage?"

"Great," I said.

The hay was dusty so I asked whether I might have a kettle of boiling water. "To scald it," I explained. "Otherwise Sandpiper might get a cough or even bronchitis or asthma."

"I'll fetch my other half," the landlord said.

49

His dumpy, grey-haired wife told me Tina must sleep with Sandpiper. "We don't allow dogs inside," she said. "And we like people to pay in advance here."

"No problem," I replied imitating the man at our corner newsagents in London. I opened my wallet. "How much?"

"Don't charge her for the pony," the landlord said.

Half an hour later, with Sandpiper and Tina, fed and watered, I sat in the inn's front parlour, the only customer, eating a plate of bacon and eggs with fresh peas, thin white bread and butter. Afterwards I devoured a large slice of apple pie lashed with cream, and no food ever tasted better. Although my mind could not free itself of words, which seemed to threaten me: - *I'll see Carey doesn't cause any problems; people have them at night and don't know anything about it next morning; I'll forbid you to ride Sandpiper* - sleep came in great waves, until my head dropped into my pudding bowl and a muddled dream started.

Eventually the landlady woke me. "It's being out all day in the fresh air," she said, "I'm the same myself. You'd best go to bed straight away, dear."

In my little attic bedroom, whose tiny window looked over the hills to the blue line of the sea, I took my tablet, crawled into a narrow bed and slept, without dreaming.

I wakened refreshed, but angry with myself for not leaving a note for Mungo. Would he contact the mainland police when he found Sandpiper had been away all night? I borrowed paper, pen and an envelope from the landlord and wrote the crofter a letter, saying I had gone to Fort William, which his wife - he was illiterate - would read to him. Then I remembered that everyone on the island knows when anybody goes anywhere, so someone would have told him that Sandpiper and I had caught the ferry. All the same, wanting to put his mind at rest, I bought a stamp from the landlord's wife and posted my letter in the box a hundred yards up the road. I tried Granny again, but there was still no reply, which was odd, because she had travelled widely in her youth and rarely went away now.

Then the landlord called me to breakfast and I ate a huge bowl of porridge, followed by scrambled eggs, baps and scones, washed down with weak tea. Afterwards - it should have been before, but sad to say, it wasn't - I fed Tina on her complete dog food, and hoped Sandpiper would survive on the nuts from my pocket and the great heap of scalded hay he had eaten during the night. Then I mucked out his stable. Would Steve or Hannah come searching for me?

The thought nagged at the back of my mind, as I rode on through rain and wind, with Tina hating the weather but following obediently at Sandpiper's heels. And if they found me? What then? They couldn't force me to return to the cottage, now that I had both my vital tablets and my animals with me. But since I was no longer riding towards Fort William, if they believed my note, and it was a big *if,* they would take another road. On foot? Or in a hired car? Or did they have a car already, hidden on the mainland, in which to take away whatever they had hidden in my parents' chest?

The questions raced through my brain, like worker bees on their way back to the hive; only the bees would have carried nectar, while my thoughts carried fear.

CHAPTER NINE

When a driver hooted behind me, I jumped, thinking it was Steve but, seeing it was the inn's landlord, I stopped and dismounted.

"Have I left something behind?"

"Not your fault," he said, getting out of the car. "My other half forgot to give you this. Here..." He held out a packed lunch. "Made it specially for you."

"Oh thank you, thank you very much."

I dug in my purse. "How much do I owe you?"

The man waved a lean dismissive arm. "On the house," he said. "She didn't want you to go hungry. She's put in a couple of biscuits for the dog."

"Great," I said. "Please thank her. I'm so grateful, really I am."

"Good luck," he said. "Keep your chin up."

He jumped back into his car, turned it in a gateway and sped off the way he had come. Watching him go, I thought how easy it is to misjudge people, for I had been certain the landlord's wife disliked me. Mean, I had unfairly decided, wouldn't give a penny to a blind man. And of course, I had been totally wrong. The delicious packed lunch was too big for my pockets so I had to untie the sleeping bag and put it with the provisions which were left from my purchases the day before.

The rain cleared as I rode on, and pale sunlight touched the hills with gold; but today I was destined first to ride through deep forests, whose darkness depressed me, until after an hour, we came out again into a land of undulating hills and white crofts and, sitting by a burn, I shared my lunch with Tina, while Sandpiper grazed. This time I remembered to water my animals before they ate. Then I bought pony nuts from a farm for Sandpiper, who being a good-doer luckily needs little food to keep fit.

Looking at the map, I realised that we must now take a main road, because the smaller ones only led to cottages or homesteads or went in circles. Tina was used to London traffic, but I knew that Sandpiper, having grown up in Mull, might find articulated lorries and high-sided vehicles terrifying. I knew, too, that frightened ponies are happier with a rider at their head rather than in the saddle, so I used Sandpiper's headcollar rope as a lead for Tina and walked along the arterial road leading both my animals, while caravans, cars, buses and lorries, raced or ground by, wearing down all our nerves. When any of them backfired or belched smoke it was all I could do to hold Sandpiper, while Tina hated the hiss of air brakes. Soon I grew hot, my legs ached and sweat ran down by face and tasted salty on my lips.

Then suddenly my dislike of the traffic turned to

hatred for my parents for leaving me on the island while they pursued their careers as writers. I told myself I was an unwanted child. (Once, you see, I had travelled with them, but now I was a responsibility they could do without) and self pity, the most useless of all emotions, held me in its grip.

When tears smarted behind my eyes and my throat felt as though sandpaper had cleaned my tonsils, I left the road for a narrow lane that led to a small farm where I asked a man shifting pig manure whether I could sleep that night in one of his barns. He said I couldn't, so I asked whether there were any bed and breakfast places around, but he turned his back on me without another word. So I dragged my unwilling animals back to that awful road, which now left the valley and climbed up through a mountain pass. Coming down the other side we passed small houses and bungalows, whose offers of accommodation had been turned round to say, "NO VACANCIES", or simply "FULL". When a crowd of motor cyclists roared by us, and, in a moment of madness I thought I saw Steve among them, I decided I had endured all I could that day. I turned off at the next side road, sat down by a burn and gave Tina a tin of dog meat, Sandpiper the few pony nuts I had kept back, and myself the remaining cheese and a bap left over from the lunch pack. Where, I silently asked the empty sky, am I to spend the night? Now whenever I tried to look at the map, Sandpiper yanked angrily at the reins, while Tina lay flat out on the verge and went to sleep. Eventually I remembered Mum's and Granny's homilies, and: *keep right on to the end of the road (from a song); if at first you don't succeed, try, try again, and Never say die...*

"What do I want to do - go back to the island to be controlled by Hannah?" I asked myself.

Then I spotted a shop a few yards down the side road, and there I bought more food and asked where I might find a bed for the night.

"Try the Minister, yonder," the woman behind the counter said: "You'll be safe with him and his wee wife."

But at the Manse a stout woman in an apron said, "noo, noo, we have no rooms to let," and shut the door.

Then the rain came down so hard that Sandpiper bowed his head before the wind and walked crabwise, Tina's tail went down between her soaking legs and I buttoned my anorak up to the top. Perhaps that saying, "It's always darkest before dawn", has some truth in it, for at this very moment of misery I saw a dilapidated shed standing in a forsaken field with waist-high pasture. As I dragged open a broken gate, Sandpiper rudely pushed past me, treading on my toes, and flinging his head down, started to guzzle the grass. Opening the shed door I met the nasty smell of musty hay, old straw and chicken droppings, but Tina dived inside and lay down gratefully, while Sandpiper's snaffle turned green with chewed grass. Then I turned my pony free and checked the fencing of the field. I drank at an old pump and saw that a water trough was full. Sandpiper rolled, and rolled again, Tina sighed contently amongst the chicken droppings.

"I am a tramp," I said aloud, because sometimes the sound of your own voice can dispel loneliness, "but tired and fed-up. Here, Tina," I broke into and shared with her a bar of chocolate, untied my sleeping bag, brushed my hair after drying it with my spare jersey - I had forgotten to bring a towel. I took off my jodphur boots and anorak, shook out dusty straw to make myself a bed, piled the contents of the sleeping bag in a corner, then slipped inside its dry interior, shut my eyes and went fast asleep.

CHAPTER TEN

I dreamt that Steve had pinned my arms behind my back. "She has fits," he said.

"She's mad, off her rocker," cried Hannah. "Tickle, tickle, little twit, I'm going to scratch your face. Scars, Carey, scars for life."

"Go away," I screamed into the darkness. But the scratching grew worse, as little clawed feet scuttled over my nose, across my cheek and away. I forced my heavy lids to open, dragged myself out of a tangled web of dreams. Feeling the prickliness of the straw, smelling the stale mustiness that hung in the air like dust, I tried to remember where I was. In our London flat or the cottage?

"Mum? Tina?"

The dog came, smelling disgustingly of old chicken droppings and reality slapped me in the face like a cold flannel. Steve and Hannah were the dream, scampering rats the awful truth. This shed was their breeding ground, their home and I the invader. As my eyes adjusted to the dark, the blackness turned to grey charcoal and I could see them everywhere, long tailed, brown, lean and eager as whippets.

"Tina."

She snuggled up against me, and despite her smell, I said, "Stay near!"

Trembling, I touched my cheeks and thought wildly of rodent diseases; an animal lover who sometimes considered becoming a naturalist, had been despicably turned sick by the sight of rats. Oh Carey!

"You should have protected me," I told Tina, wanting to blame someone other than myself. "If you were a terrier..." but she was looking at the roof where the rain beat a wild tattoo and water dripped through holes and here and there a thread of the dawn sky was visible.

I started to shout at the rats, but clearly I was a novelty for whom they felt no fear. When a large male appeared from a pocket in my anorak I threw a handful of straw at him. "Get away, go!" And my words must have wakened some basic instinct in Tina, because she jumped up and started to herd them, barking and snapping, towards the door and in moments every rat had disappeared through one of a myriad holes.

Now, as the rain slowed down, I heard Sandpiper tearing at the long grass and knew I would have to ride slowly at first, because he would have overeaten. And then a shaft of light, fragile and grey as gossamer, came through the shed's window and remembering my tablet, I picked my way across the floor to my anorak, dug in its pocket and screamed as a rat jumped out and ran up my arm. Panicking, I opened the shed door and ran outside to be met by fresh air as soothing as a long cool drink on a hot day. Like a stable boy of long ago I went to the pump to wash my hair and face in cold water. I took off my clothes and shook them, and Sandpiper came to nuzzle my pockets, so then I returned to the shed for polo mints I had bought for him at the local shop. This time I shook my anorak before plunging a hand into a pocket. The last of the chocolate had been taken by the rats, but the mints were still there and my tablets, but not my wallet, my wallet, oh where was my wallet? I felt the blood draining again from my face; my legs weakening. Keep calm, Carey, keep calm, and then I saw it lying in the straw with a trail of paper leading from it to a hole in the floor - my fifty pound notes torn and taken for bedding.

"Oh no, Tina, no!"

I wanted to scream, to throw myself down and kick like a thwarted toddler, but what use would that be? Instead I started crawling distastefully on my hands and knees picking up fragments of paper in the hope that I might turn them into one note. Before long I had managed to collect enough to make the Queen's face, but her crown was missing and the Bank of England, had disappeared down a rat hole. One hundred pounds gone for ever and how bizarre, I thought, trying to see the comic side, that the rats have taken only the most valuable notes. Feeling calmer, I washed my hands again at the pump and cleaned my teeth, and threw two packets of nibbled biscuits and one of crisps for the birds, after Tina and Sandpiper, tasting rat, had spat them out.

I brushed my own and Tina's hair to rid us of the rodent and chicken smells, groomed Sandpiper, repacked my sleeping bag, tacked up and headed again for the main road.

Riding on, I imagined Granny's comments, "What's a hundred pounds these days. Business people spend it on a dinner for two or an evening's drinking and Cosmo ..." Here she would pause as she always did when mentioning my father, because I was his daughter and she didn't want to fuel any rift that might grow between us. "Yes, Cosmo earns far more than that for just ten minutes on TV."

Then, I thought, Granny would ask after the golden eagles, and when I told her I had seen them, she would wave her arms as she always did when she was excited, and say, "What an experience!"

Had Granny met Hannah? Probably yes, I decided, because she had known Hannah's mother, long before my father came on the scene, which was perhaps the reason Mum told me Granny was the key? I looked at my watch, which said half past five - four hours, I thought, before I can try phoning again.

Now the main road was gloriously empty; cocks crowed and the wind whispered in the myrtle and the rowans, below a sky whose delicate rain-washed cleanness made me wish I could paint; and all the earth smelt good. My tummy rumbled with hunger, but my worries drifted away, as I revelled in the loveliness of the world around me and Sandpiper's long easy stride. I would manage without the hundred pounds, because surely justice was on my side and the gods were, therefore with me.

CHAPTER ELEVEN

I thought I should always ride at this time in the morning, partly because there was so little traffic and partly because Steve and Hannah were unlikely to look for me so early. They would, I decided, be anxious to lay their hands on me, because they had no idea how much or how little I knew about their activities. How much had I heard of Steve's telephone conversation? Did I eavesdrop for long outside the door while they - the gang - pored over the map and discussed routes? Had I been a better detective, I would have posed a greater threat, but they were not to know that, sadly, I had been too busy thinking about my own personal problems to be cool and sensible. At this very moment Hannah might be trembling in her Doc Marten boots at the thought of the harm I might do her.

My thoughts were interrupted by a clatter of hoofs, as a red haired woman on a dappled grey approached.

"Good heavens!" she cried. "Someone else with the same idea. Isn't it absolutely super at this time of day?

And what a smashing collie."

"I couldn't face the traffic and I've a long way to go," I said, suddenly very pleased to have someone to talk to.

"May I ride along with you? Where are you going?"

"Yorkshire."

"Yorkshire! I don't believe it. You're joking. Anyway, darling," my new friend continued, "Your little pony isn't going to get there at this rate. Cos those dinky little hoofs need shoes?"

"Yes, but I've lost one hundred pounds," I blurted out, suddenly near tears, and then the whole story of the rats poured from my tongue like seeds from a broken packet.

"We turn off here," the woman said when I had finished. "Darling, I don't know whether to believe you or not. The whole thing is just too, too fantastic."

"I know," I said, "But if I had wanted to invent, I would have thought up a more credible story, wouldn't I?"

"Darling, you're so sweet; come back with me," my companion cried, "It's only five miles to go and more or less in your direction. I need cheering up, a break, or I shall die. What's your name, but the way?"

"Carey."

"Carey," she rolled the name round her mouth, like someone tasting a sweet for the first time. "Nice, different, and the other half?"

I hesitated, and she said, "No lies."

"Mancroft," I used my grandmother's surname.

"This way then, Carey Mancroft," the woman said,

turning down a side road just as a lorry approached. "I'm Elspeth Macdonald, by the way, spelt with a small c, unlike the hamburger chain. Shall we trot?"

We spoke little as we rode the five miles to her house, which turned out to be huge and castellated, with a sweeping drive and a stable block with a clock and weather vane.

"Too big for just me," Elspeth said, leaping nimbly from the saddle. "Oh look, a light's on, Nanny's up. Great."

"Do I perplex you?" she asked a few minutes later as we bedded down a loose-box for Sandpiper, before giving Tina food and water.

"No, no," I replied, and then on the spur of the moment, added, "No more than I perplex you," and filling a haynet, she said, "I love that."

Nanny, a sickle-backed old woman with poor, arthritic hands, met us on the doorstep.

"Coffee's on the table," she said.

"Excellent," cried Elspeth. "Nanny, I found this little stray girl riding all alone on the big road. She slept in a shed, has no money and needs a bath."

"I do have some money," I said.

"Always exaggerate," Elspeth advised, "Exaggeration oils the wheels of life."

"Your father rang," Nanny said, as we walked across the flagged hall, "Wanting to know how you were."

"And what did you say?"

"Out riding," I told him, "and in good health as far as I could see."

"I had a breakdown," Elspeth explained to me. "Look,

there's a loo, and after breakfast you're to have a bath."

"Do I smell?"

"Sort of."

"Sorry."

"Don't apologise, darling. It's all very novel for me, a little bit of drama, and I need drama like a bear needs honey, don't I, Nanny dear?"

"Yes," the old woman said.

By now we had reached a small, sunlit room, where a round table stood laden with every kind of bap, roll and scone.

"Sit down, Carey, make yourself at home. Nanny will lay a place for you and bring us porridge."

"Can't I help?" I asked, terribly embarrassed to find myself waited on by an old woman.

"No, no, she loves it," hissed Elspeth. "It gives point to her life. Now in a minute we'll phone the farrier, a super man, and he'll be round like greased lightning with his portable forge."

I pulled out my wallet. "How much does he charge?" I asked.

"Don't worry darling, Daddy will pay."

"Thanks, but he doesn't even know me," I objected, plunging a spoon into my steaming hot porridge.

"Daddy's a millionaire," replied Elspeth, smugly, "Or, to be more accurate, he's married an American millionairess, so no problem, eat, drink and be merry," she smiled at me as though we had entered into a joint conspiracy, and I noticed for the first time the wild look in her sea-green eyes, the impetuous mouth and the beauty of her red hair.

"I am an actress," she told me, after I had bathed and she had lent me jeans and a tee shirt because Nanny had stolen away my clothes to wash, "And I married a darling man, a jewel without price, but nutty as a fruit cake. And heavens, did we have fun? Yes, sir! You name it, we did it. Crazy we were, totally, absolutely crazy! Tight as ticks from morning till night. And then Daddy" - now she strutted about the room, puffing out her cheeks and pretending to be her father - "Daddy came to the rescue. He brought me back from the States to this God-forsaken place which, my dear, he owns, and got me treatment."

"Treatment?"

"Yes, darling, I hit the bottle and I guess he loves me ... shocked?"

"Of course not."

"So dear Nanny, who brought me up, is back in business and I've returned to my first love - horses. But, darling, I'm bored rigid, so do me a favour and stay a little, at least until I see my psychologist tomorrow. And, by the way, I do, do, do believe your story about the rats - your clothes and Nanny's expression. Ugh!" Elspeth touched her nose." But such a bizarre story, I love it. When I'm better I shall dine out on it; so, my little stray kitten, let's see if dear Cluny Macpherson, who is named after the great man of Jacobite fame, is on his way to shoe your wee pony."

"You've phoned him?"

"While you were in your bath."

And so I found myself swept onwards on the tide of Elspeth's enthusiasm into another day without Steve or Hannah finding me.

CHAPTER TWELVE

How astonishing, I thought when I wakened in a four poster bed, one night in a rat-infested shed, the next here. And, being a convent school girl, I thanked my guardian angel.

Tina who had been lent a dog's basket for the night got up and stretched.

"No, don't get on the bed," I told her. "Down, down," for the white sheets were lace-trimmed and the quilt old patchwork. I jumped up and saw that Sandpiper had been turned out in the small park which surrounded the house and its gardens, which were somewhat overgrown. My room's walls were lined in watered silk paper - the American's choice, I decided.

I took my pill and dressed in Elspeth's jeans and tee shirt and shyly went down to find she was back from an early ride on her grey, Justin. Nanny hovered anxiously while a sumptuous breakfast with smoked haddock awaited us in the small room, which faced East across a terrace.

"Aren't you going to eat with us?" I asked Nanny.

"Oh noo," she said. "I shall be bringing you your clothes the next minute."

She came back with them neatly folded over one arm. "And here are the wee things you left in your pocket." She laid on the table: a packet, which had held the peanuts and two receipts from the shops where I had bought provisions.

"How bizarre," exclaimed Elspeth, "The writing on that packet is in Spanish. You didn't tell me you'd been to Spain, Carey."

"No, Tina fished it out of Scottish waters," I explained what had happened. "Do they speak Spanish in the Philippines?" I asked.

"I guess so," Elspeth said and then, as her face hardened, "You must leave right now, Carey. I'm working on a book, so I'll be busy. No more time for tall stories."

"Can I just try Granny once more?" I asked.

"Go ahead," Elspeth said in a voice so bored that I could hardly believe she was the woman I had met yesterday. On my way to the telephone Nanny caught up with me. "It's one of her bad days," she said, touching my arm. "They come like that after a good one. I've put all your things together in the hall. You'd best change and be going soon."

An elderly, unfamiliar voice answered Granny's phone.

"Mrs Mancroft's away, I'm just minding the house," it said.

"This is Carey, her granddaughter. I'm riding down from Scotland to see her.

69

"I can't hear you," the old lady said.

"When can I speak to her, please?"

"She's at the hospital, visiting."

"Who? Is someone ill?"

"I'm sorry, dear, I can't hear."

"Please tell her Carey rang," I shouted.

And then the phone went down the other end.

"Off you go now!" shouted Elspeth standing in the hall, a new and sinister light in her green eyes, which made the hairs on my arms stand up. Nanny handed me a packet of sandwiches and, remembering a story called Dr Jekyll and Mr Hyde, about a man with a split personality, I picked up my things and ran. Poor Elspeth is unstable, I thought, she leaps from happiness to despair, from liking to hatred.

Then suddenly, the world seemed a much more difficult place than I had ever imagined, and my luck in meeting her when she was in an enthusiastic mood quite extraordinary. As I tacked up Sandpiper, I hoped Elspeth really did have a wealthy father, who would pay the farrier, but, just in case she didn't, I decided to ask my parents to send Mr Macdonald a cheque. I would post the Nanny a present, too, and write to thank Elspeth.

The night before Elspeth had shown me on a map several tracks I could take to avoid roads. First, she said, I must head for a loch. And by nine o'clock I had reached it, a rippling lake of water, fringed with larch and pine. Little clouds sailed like dinghies across an azure sky, so beautiful that my dismal thoughts fled, Sandpiper, inspired, too, stopped to gaze into the hills,

Tina ran to and fro as though intoxicated by her own energy, for this was one of those magical places which lift the spirits of all but the most unfeeling people. Here, Steve and Hannah no longer mattered. I had escaped and if they were smuggling drugs that was their affair.

At last, I thought, I was free of worry and handling my own life and a long sunny day stretched before me and then a sight brought me with a jerk to my senses: a man with a rucksack on his back was waving to me as he walked down a hill path. Coming closer, he called "Could it be that you are Carey Lovegrove?" and, my wits sharpened by fear, I shouted back, "no, I'm Susan Smith."

"Do you ken any lassie of that name? It's important I'm told," he said on reaching me.

"Never heard of her," I replied, half-ashamed again that lies flowed so effortlessly from my tongue.

"What would ye be doing then?"

"Riding. I'm a friend of Elspeth Macdonald."

"Och aye, from the big house."

"Has someone asked you to look for this Carey what's-it, then?"

"A man on yon hill," he pointed vaguely. "She's in need of medicine."

"Sorry, I can't help," I said, and rode on, weak at the knees.

So Steve or someone else was in pursuit, and what would they do if they caught up with me?

71

CHAPTER THIRTEEN

I was munching one of Nanny's delicious smoked salmon sandwiches, as I rode, and Tina was sniffing for rabbits in a ditch, when a policeman in a patrol car drew up beside me.

"Excuse me, Miss," he began politely. " Is there a chance you might be the young lassie, Carey Lovegrove?"

My full mouth gave me a moment to think, while I chewed and swallowed the last morsel of the sandwich.

"Carey Lovegrove." Now it was my turn to roll the name round my mouth. "No, I'll not be knowing her."

He looked me up and down. "She's travelling with a collie and a chestnut pony, but yours ...?"

"Dun," I said, "with black points."

"Has she done something bad?" I asked, while desperately willing Tina to stay in the ditch.

"No, no, she's been reported as a missing person, ran away from home they say. Mentally handicapped."

"That's not me," I said. "I shall be taking ten GCSEs

72

next year."

"A' weel, thank you for your help." He drove away, and a moment later Tina came out of the ditch.

What luck, I thought, that Steve's descriptions were so inaccurate and that I am tall for my age. But supposing the police go to see Elspeth, whom I have told, not all, but too much, and I am caught and taken to a children's home? Well, Granny, I told myself, will sort it out. And perhaps the police will search the cottage, and take Steve and Hannah away in handcuffs. My spirits rose at that hope, as I took a hill track, which I wrongly thought Elspeth had pointed at on her map. Here, guided by the sun alone, I was lost in a myriad of sheep paths. Then, miraculously, I came back to the right road and, for the rest of the day, rode down the valley Elspeth had suggested, where cars of sight-seers passed me by and occasionally a lorry, and Tina kept obediently at Sandpiper's heels, while all the time I was watching out for Steve.

When the shadows lengthened I rested under a tree. Sandpiper grazed and I gave Tina the biscuits Nanny had thoughtfully packed for her. I found a post office and shop in the next village, open late because it was run by Asians, and bought bread and cheese and a bar of chocolate. I asked for a glass of water and mixed Tina's complete dog food with it on the picnic plate. Afterwards, not wanting to spend the twenty eight pounds, which was all I had left, I started to look for fields or copses where we might find shelter, for I longed to sleep out under the stars, an experience loved by my parents and I knew that in the depths of the countryside I would feel safe.

But, even as I imagined myself snug in my sleeping bag under a tree, clouds rolled across the sky, a wind rose, and soft rain blew like smoke across the valley. Then, just as my hopes were sinking, I saw a castle on a hillside, a ruin of pepperpot towers, dramatic yet forlorn in their decay. It was empty; its walls coated with lichen and moss; its ground floor carpeted in grass, its broken roof a home for weeds, but happily the green land around it was fenced. I pushed open an iron farm gate.

"Quick inside. Through we go, Stand!"

Sandpiper threw his head down to eat the short green pasture, while I whisked off his saddle and the awkward-shaped sleeping bag, untied his headcollar from around his neck and, took off his bridle.

A stone staircase led to the castle's first floor, partly protected by the remains of a roof above, where I chose to sleep, for now the stars would be hidden by clouds and I needed protection from the wind and rain. I unpacked my sleeping bag, shook out the clothes inside, ate half the bread and cheese and decided, that if the drizzle stopped, I would walk down to the river below to drink, for Scotland's river water is mostly wonderfully clean. I put my clothes back into the bottom of my sleeping bag, took a tablet, crawled inside, and slept.

I dreamt I had reached Granny's cottage and found it empty. An old man, bent as a mountain tree, told me she had gone to Mongolia to be with her daughter. Then, turning suddenly into a tough young policeman, he arrested me; he took me to a cell and ordered me to confess. Confess to what? My question turned him into the Mother Superior at my Convent School, a stern woman, with gold rimmed glasses perched on her nose and hands so still that she might be a statue. Tina's growl interrupted the interview. The cell left my mind. I could see a star. The smell of wood smoke and the sound of voices and footsteps drifted up to my hideaway. I put a hand round Tina's mouth to stop her growling and hissed, "Quiet, sit!"

Then I edged towards a gap in the wall and looked down to where four campers sat round a fire cooking sausages: two men and two women in anoraks.

And Sandpiper? I crept bent double, across those ramparts, past notices saying Danger until I knew the worst - the gate was wide open and Sandpiper had gone. It was two o'clock in the morning when depression comes easily and I cried.

Presently I saw that the campers had a van and, calming down, I toyed with the idea of suggesting they jumped in it at once and drove me round until I had retrieved the pony they had so carelessly let out, but what would they think of a young girl sleeping all alone in a ruined castle? Would they really swallow the Duke of Edinburgh Award story? I sat for a long time with my arms wrapped around myself not knowing what to do. Then I decided to tell them everything and ask for help. I climbed slowly to my feet, went back to the hole in the masonry and looked down. They were drinking wine. Suddenly afraid, I turned back to my sleeping bag and drifted into troubled sleep.

CHAPTER FOURTEEN

When morning came and the campers still slept in their tents, I stood on the ramparts again and looked in all directions. But there was no sign of Sandpiper and this, I thought, was one of the worst moments of my life.

Everybody knows that lone girls are at risk from murderers and maniacs, but on a pony I had felt safe. Now I would have to be on my guard all the time. And supposing Sandpiper was killed by a truck on the road? I pushed that thought straight from my mind. I found I had two bread rolls left and gave one to Tina and ate the other myself. I took my tablet. Then I went down to the river and had a long drink before washing the picnic plate and mug.

The sun was rising on a bed of pink and gold clouds: *Red morning, Shepherd's warning.* If that were true there would be rain before nightfall, and I should get wet again. For the first time I felt like abandoning the journey, for this morning I had wakened stiff as an old dog, and my legs still ached abominably.

"Don't be a wimp, Carey," I told myself in Mum's

voice. "Never say die," in Granny's, "Where there's life there's hope," in Dad's. And "I can handle it," in mine. And I thought how lucky I was to have all my limbs and perfect eyes and ears, while some teenagers were disabled and confined to wheelchairs. And, I thought - overdoing it a bit - there are poor babies born with flippers for hands and feet. So why am I moaning? Quelling self pity, I put the plate and mug, with my change of clothes, used map, tin opener and toothpaste and brush, back in the sleeping bag, which I rolled up again and attached to the saddle. I tied Sandpiper's headcollar round my waist, clipped its rope on Tina's collar - one lost animal was enough - put the saddle over one arm and the bridle over the other and set off, leading Tina.

Which way did Sandpiper go? Left or right, north or south? Probably north, heading back to the island, I decided but, stubbornly reluctant to retrace by steps, I walked south. A young Englishman passed me on a cycle. "Lost your horse?"

"That's right. Have you seen him?"

"Ride him cowboy."

He pedalled away, laughing as though he had made a great joke and, irritated by his stupidity, I quickened my step and only stopped now and then to look across fields and moorland, and my arms ached and my legs felt weighted down with lead.

Then I heard a car behind me, and looking back, saw a cheery pipe smoker at the wheel and children and a dog on the back seat.

"Can we help?" the man spoke with a warm northern accent. "Fallen off?"

"No. Someone left a gate open and he's escaped."

"Oh dear, oh dear. You look done-in, want a lift?"

I looked at the children and the black labrador and decided the man was safe.

"Thanks."

A small girl jumped out. "You can sit with uz," she said. Mr Brown put my tack and the sleeping bag in the boot.

"I'm afraid my dog will want to come, too."

"She can sit on the floor with Mick," the driver said, "My name's Brown, what's yours?"

"Carey Mancroft," I replied and could have kicked myself for not saying Susan Smith.

"Now tell us where you've been looking, Carey?" Mr Brown sounded wonderfully matter of fact.

"Just along this road. I must have walked two miles," I said.

"No wonder you look fagged out," observed Mr Brown. "Well then, we'll turn round and go in the opposite direction. I think that will be favourite."

And from then on I felt at home with the Browns, because the lovely postman in Granny's village uses *favourite* all the time and he always says uz instead of us.

"Thanks a lot."

"What's your dog called," the youngest girl asked. And then we all talked at once about dog and animal names.

"Like a buttered bun?" Mr Brown said.

"Oh yes, please," shrieked his three little girls, who

were called Emma, Clare and Tracey.

"I was asking Carey, not you lot," he said. "They're old, mind. Mother forgot to take them out last night." Gobbling buns, I was so happy to be with friendly people again that for a few moments I almost forgot about Sandpiper.

We drove up every side road, every lane, every track, but saw no sign of him.

"Disappeared into thin air," said Mr Brown. "Could anyone want to steal him like?"

"He's not a show pony," I said.

We returned to the main road and, as we drove along at around fifty miles an hour, a motor cyclist sped past at high speed, wearing an old fashioned, open-faced helmet.

"A right fool!" exclaimed Mr Brown. "Look at him. Does he want to get killed?"

And, at the same moment, I saw the fool was Steve, his eyes reddened by the wind, his straggly hair plastered against his narrow head. Supposing he found Sandpiper before we did?

"Motor bikes stink," Clare said.

"And what do your Mum and Dad think about you being out on your own?" asked Mr Brown. "Do you live far from here or what?"

Then I had to spin again my story about the Duke of Edinburgh Award. "A sort of survival test," I finished, and Mr Brown asked me whether I went to Gordonstoun, which is a Scottish school, specialising in making its pupils tough and self reliant, and I said, "No I'm taught by nuns mostly."

"So long as you're not running away from home or something daft like that."

"Oh no, of course not. Anyway, I'm adult now," I replied, glad once again that I had grown so fast the last year that I looked seventeen.

Then suddenly we all saw Sandpiper standing, on the verge of a side road, looking very sweet and rather forlorn. "Is that him?"

"Yes," I cried, and my eyes filled with tears of relief. "Please stop."

"No way, there's a car right on my tail. I'll turn round further up," said Mr Brown.

"He's resting a foreleg, that's serious," I said.

"He's brilliant," chorused the three girls, while Tina stood on her hindlegs to see out of the window.

A few moment later I slipped the headcollar on Sandpiper and ran my hands down his legs "He has a puncture between his tendons," I told the girls who now hovered round me like moths by a light. "He needs a tetanus injection and an antibiotic."

"And where shall we find a vet, luv?" asked Mr Brown. "You're in a bit of a pickle, Carey, aren't you?"

"I'm so relieved he hasn't been hit by a car," I said. "Nothing else really matters at the moment."

"I saw a pub, further back," Emma, the eldest girl, said, "We could ask there."

"Quick thinking," I said.

"Yes, that'll be favourite," Mr Brown declared. "Into the car girls, and Mick, too. Come on, no messing about. See you Carey."

I stood, hoping Steve would not return and spot me,

while Sandpiper dozed and Tina scratched around a rabbit burrow. Then in less than ten minutes, the Browns were back, their faces wreathed in smiles.

"A quarter of a mile down the road, a Mr George Campbell. We'd best hurry because he shuts at half past twelve," said Mr Brown.

"Great. Thank you so much for all your help."

"You've not got rid of us yet," Mr Brown joked.

"You're our holiday adventure," Clare added. "It's brilliant."

CHAPTER FIFTEEN

Mr Campbell, a short man with pitch black hair, was kind and efficient. When he heard I was trying for a Duke of Edinburgh Award, he said he wouldn't charge me a consultation fee. He injected Sandpiper with anti-tetanus serum and penicillin. He cleaned the puncture, squeezed in antibiotic ointment and, finally, protected the leg with a strong, waterproof bandage, which he said I could take off after three days.

"You've got a bonnie pony with an excellent constitution, perfect for long-distance riding," he told me. "Rest him today and carry on tomorrow."

"How much do I owe you?" I brought out my wallet.

"Ten pounds," he replied, and then, when he saw I had only two ten pound notes, he said, "No, make it five." And smiled when he saw the relief on my face.

"You got it dirt cheap," commented Mr Brown, as I put a bridle on Sandpiper. "Now look, see that signpost there? - well, take the left turn and then second right and second left and you'll see our white holiday cottage. The Rowans, the name's on the gate, you can't miss it."

"But," I began...

"And I don't want any argument, you're spending the night with uz, isn't she girls?"

"Yes," shrieked his daughters like an audience at a pantomime supporting the principal boy.

"It looks like another wet day, so we need a diversion," Mr Brown added. "The dog can ride with uz."

"But Sandpiper ..."

"I'll talk to the neighbours. They've got a holiday let with an orchard. By the time you arrive everything will be sewn-up." Mr Brown assured me.

And it was.

"What you need, luv," Mrs Brown a plump blonde with permed hair, said, "Is a nice hot bath."

Behind her hovered Shaun, her cousin's son, she told me. His parents had parted, so the kind Browns had invited him to share their holiday.

"Can you play backgammon?" he asked.

"No sorry," I said.

"Want me to teach you?"

"Brilliant, after the bath."

"We want you to play Scrabble with uz," Emma and Clare objected.

"No, dominoes," shrieked Tracey, the youngest.

"We'll take it in turns," I said. "All right?"

Soaking in the bath, I thought Mum had been right when she told me that life for some people was made up of bad luck and good luck, while others coasted through on the level. "You," she said, "are accident prone. You attract strange situations and so you'll have lots of ups and downs, just like Cosmo and me."

But I decided, pulling out the plug, poor Elspeth can't help her see-saws, because she's probably been born with the wrong genes.

Later Shaun, who was fair-haired, hazel-eyed and talkative, suggested I was lonely, riding by myself.

"Not really. Tina and Sandpiper are great company," I assured him.

"Then you must be like me, a lone wolf," he said, and laughed.

Every time we looked at each other we laughed, and though he beat me easily at backgammon I didn't care. Anyway, I later beat him at Scrabble. And, as the day passed, I wished I could stay for ever and Sandpiper, despite an occasional neigh for Morag, seemed happy in the orchard. Mrs Brown cooked us a lunch, with roast lamb and apple suet pudding, and Mr Brown drove five miles to get a takeaway supper. So, I am sorry to say, it wasn't until the evening that I remembered to phone Granny. And once again, there was no reply. What was going on? The question nagged me for a moment and then Shaun started to tell me about his parents' marriage break-up and poor Granny went on my back burner again.

Tracey and Clare shared a bed that night, so there was a spare one for me in Emma's room, where she and I talked for an hour, mostly about our schools.

Downstairs Mr and Mrs Brown watched TV, and before long I heard Dad's voice, in a Repeat, as he hosted a quiz show, and I was glad then that nobody knew my true name, because sometimes the fact that I am Dad's daughter affects people's feelings towards me. When Emma slept, Hannah's voice hissed again in my ear: "People have them at night and don't know anything about it next morning." Supposing Hannah spoke the truth and it happened again and Emma saw? It was an awful thought, but then I remembered the specialist had never mentioned night-time attacks to me, being more worried about stress. Now, a tablet taken and a good supper inside me, I felt totally relaxed. Don't believe that snake, I told myself in Granny's voice, just before sleep blotted out all my anxieties.

Next morning after breakfast Shaun helped me groom Sandpiper, using Mick's brush, and I found myself telling him about my black-outs.

"Just a tiny fault in an electrical impulse in the brain's computer," he said, airily, "And I expect they'll soon find a cure, it's called epilepsy, by the way."

"How do you know?"

"Mum's a doctor and, being Irish, a great talker. She brings her worries home and wants me to go into medicine, too, but I don't know ..."

"Why not?"

"Not clever enough. Maybe I'll be a drifter," he said. "Wow, some tail," he exclaimed, as he brushed Sandpiper's, which is thick and black. "What corkscrews! If only we were still in the days of horsehair mattresses you would make a small fortune."

"Oh Christmas! I've forgotten my tablet." I dropped my dandy brush.

"I don't suppose once in a while will make any difference," Shaun said.

"You'd be surprised," I shouted as I rushed indoors to get the bottle out of my anorak pocket.

I returned to find a languid woman from next door complaining that Sandpiper had bitten the top off a young tree, and I thought: *here comes bad luck again*.

"Are you the pony's owner? I tell you, Mr Young, who owns the cottage, will be furious when he sees," she said.

I thought of my two crumpled ten pound notes and the loose change left after I had paid the vet, and said, "Please send the bill then."

I fetched a pen and paper and wrote down Granny's address and gave it to the woman.

"How do I know you're genuine?" she asked.

"I'll vouch for her," offered Shaun. "And you trust the Browns, don't you?"

"That's true," the woman said, inspecting my handwriting, "All right then. We'll leave it like that." And, thankfully, I remembered to shout, "sorry," as she walked away.

"You were so cool," Shaun told me.

"And you, too," I said, and we laughed again as we went back to our grooming.

CHAPTER SIXTEEN

The rain had gone; there were blue skies again and, as I rode, I sang one of Madonna's songs, although, I confess, I don't like her much as a person.

Tina had wanted to stay with the Browns and Mick. She was tired of roads and traffic, so I led her for the first mile, but now she was trotting along at Sandpiper's heels, keeping in as usual. Her exceptionally good behaviour was due not to me, but to a brilliant dog trainer, to whom my parents sent her when she was three months old while I was away at school.

This morning Sandpiper was sound; Mr Brown had gone over my route with me and lent me a map, and Mrs Brown had given me a huge pack of sandwiches and a kiss on each cheek. Tracey had cried when I left. Shaun had exchanged addresses with me and said, "Write." The fact that I had won their affection, without them knowing I was Melanie and Cosmo Lovegrove's daughter made me feel warm inside. I was standing on my own feet at last.

Then suddenly, without warning, my happiness shattered. A familiar figure sprang from a ditch and, with a leap of my heart, I came face to face with Steve.

"Carey, what do you think you're doing?"

Steve looked very seedy. His beard and hair both needed trimming; his eyes were red-rimmed; his large hands limp at his sides. I had been dreading this moment; yet now I seemed to be facing only a failure, who could do me no harm.

"Hannah is crazy with worry."

"Tough," I said. "If we're going to talk we had better get in that gateway - the traffic..."

"You're at risk ... your illness, your age...." He said when we were off the road.

"Only at risk from you and Hannah. I can handle myself. Have you reported me to the police as a missing person?"

"Unofficially, yes. Are you hoping to go to your grandmother's?"

"Of course, you wouldn't let me phone and so..."

"She's dead," said Steve, a thin smile hovering on his red lips.

"Oh no!" With a mighty effort I held back my tears, because Steve was there.

"Yeah, she died the day after Hannah came."

Then I remembered the old lady, who answered the phone at a later date, saying Mrs Mancroft was visiting someone in hospital.

"You're lying," I said. "Both you and Hannah lie."

"Have you tried calling her?"

"Yes."

"Any reply?"

I paused. Better not to tell him about the old lady,

better to let him think I was going along with his story.

"No"

"Well then. Hadn't you best come back with me? I'll hire a truck for the pony. Right?"

"Wrong." I turned Sandpiper, pushed him into a trot and continued our journey.

"What are you going to do now?" Steve yelled.

"Ride on," I shouted back.

"Dead people can't help."

"Shut up," I cried, tears falling at last - after all, the deaf lady might have been deranged by grief at Granny's death. Now Steve ran back up the road, presumably to get his motor cycle, and I saw that rarity in this part of Scotland - a bridle path.

"Come on Sandpiper, Tina heel!" We galloped along the path at breakneck speed, although at times the going was rough. After about a mile we came out on a side road, where I saw tents in a large flat field and heard a voice calling out entry numbers over a microphone. A horse show and village fete! Where better to avoid Steve?

"A big event?" I asked the man at the gate.

"Half and half, serious and not serious," he replied.

"Do I have to pay to go in?" I asked.

"Of course not." He waved a welcoming arm. "I'm only here to charge the cars."

I saw two rings, one for the experts the other for less serious competitors.

I went to the second, where riders were being gathered together for the next event.

"What is it?" I asked a jolly-looking girl on a piebald

pony.

"You're too late," she said. "Late entries closed five minutes ago. It's for the pony with the prettiest markings."

Then I wished her good luck, went to the Secretary's tent and got a programme. There was a pound entry fee for each event. I ran my eye down the next three, which were: - THE PONY WITH THE LOVELIEST EYES, THE PONY WITH THE BEST TAIL and a straight forward TROTTING RACE. I decided to enter all three, when I saw each first prize was ten pounds.

"Just a bit of fun for the bairns," the Secretary said. "This is the first time we've tried it on a Sunday."

"Am I too old?" I asked.

"Oh no, we're all bairns at heart," he said.

There were eighteen entries - and one pony I was glad to see ridden by a grown-up - for my first class. But, even as I rode into the ring, I knew a Welsh pony whose enormous dark eyes were enhanced by the whiteness of his coat would win. A fat Highland pony with tranquil eyes was second, and a Shetland third.

When it was over, I led Sandpiper to my sleeping bag, which I had left Tina to guard, dug out the dandy brush and worked on his tail.

"You should used a body brush for that," a passing expert said. "A dandy brush breaks too many hairs."

Then my number was called and we returned to the ring followed by the jolly girl on the piebald.

We were asked to go round in a large circle and then called in one by one to make a long line. I stood between a chestnut with a pulled tail and a grey whose tail had obviously been well washed. In contrast to them Sandpiper looked like a wild pony just off the moors.

The judge, a local minor film star, who knew nothing about the care of tails, asked me whether my pony kicked and when I said, "No," ran his hand through the corkscrew hairs Shaun had brushed so enthusiastically that morning.

"The prize is for the best, not the most beautiful, and best must also mean strong and long-lasting," he told the official at his side. "So I think this one has it."

"Oh thank you, thank you very much," I said.

As I cantered round, a red rosette in my mouth, I saw Steve enter the showground, wheeling his motor cycle. So, once again my good luck was to be balanced by bad.

I returned to the collecting ring and waited to be called for the trotting race.

"Your pony looks very fit," the girl on the piebald told me. "But I'm surprised you were first, because his tail carriage is nothing special."

"Really," I said, my eyes watching Steve who was approaching Tina. Supposing he stole her and my sleeping bag? Then I saw him step back as Tina snarled and at the same moment my number was called. There were six of us in the first heat, and I was lucky again, because Sandpiper saw a garron mare enter the showground and, thinking she was Morag, trotted as fast as he could in the hope of reaching her and won. While I watched the other heats

Steve came up to me.

"What are you playing at?" he asked.

"I've never ridden in a show before. It's great," I told him. "See my rosette?"

"I shall stick with you now," he said. "And if you don't play ball you could meet with a nasty accident."

"Blackmail," I said. "Something to tell the police."

There were four ponies in the final, two bays, one black and me, and the garron mare wasn't in sight.

"On your marks, get set, go!"

The black reared, one bay, who had been in harness, took the lead, his stable mate, the second bay, followed a yard behind, then Sandpiper cantered and I obeyed somebody's shout of "Turn him in a circle," which slowed me down. The black, frightened by a ringside child waving a flag, still jibbed. And his obstinacy allowed Sandpiper and me to be third past the finishing post. Then it was my turn to canter round the ring again, this time with a yellow rosette in my mouth.

"You shouldn't have won," the girl on the piebald told me. "Black Magic is a great trotter. That twit with the flag spoiled everything."

"His bad luck is my good luck," I said. "That's life."

I went to the Secretary's tent and collected my prizes: ten pounds and a bag of pony nuts, half of which I fed to Sandpiper, after I had taken him to a trough to drink. Then I shared Mrs Brown's sandwiches with Tina, watched by Steve.

CHAPTER SEVENTEEN

We were at loggerheads.

"You'll never reach Yorkshire, and what's the point if she isn't there?" asked Steve, crouching down so that he could look into my eyes.

"I shall live in Granny's cottage, if she's died," I found it hard to utter those words. "Mum will come home to sort things out. Have you thought of that?" I asked triumphantly. "Well, have you? Mum will sort you and Hannah out, too. Brilliant, I can't wait."

Seeing this possibility had not crossed Steve's mind, I felt in control. "And," I added, "If I meet with an accident, there will be an inquest and Dad will spare no money to discover the true facts. I have no doubt the medical men will know whether I had a black-out or not before ..."

"Rubbish, fantasising as usual," Steve said. "You're a sick girl, Carey. Come back, please. All is forgiven. I didn't mean it about the accident. I'm here to protect you from yourself."

"You're forgiving me. I like that."

I jumped up, and bridled Sandpiper, who had been

grazing in his headcollar.

"Where are you going now?" asked Steve.

"Mind your own business."

"It is my business. I'm here on behalf of Hannah, who your mother left in charge of you."

"And you doped me and wouldn't let me use a phone. You're here because you want to be around if I go to the police. Big joke," I said, mounting. "Tina heel."

"I can get you taken into care," Steve said.

"Right, and I'll tell them what you've been up to."

"Which is?"

"Not telling."

"Nobody will believe you, an unbalanced - adolescent girl, suffering from fits - everyone knows such people are hysterical."

"Granny will believe me."

Earlier I had glimpsed, beyond a row of cottages, moorland, which was perhaps treacherous because the summer had been so wet. Motor cycles, I thought, stick in mud more easily than ponies do.

I squeezed Sandpiper with my calves and we trotted from the showground, his bridle decorated with the rosettes, the sleeping bag heavy with pony nuts. We took the road that led to a track which wound its way into the hills. Steve rode behind me on his motor cycle, whose stink blotted out the scent of the heather and the last of the broom. When the going softened, I sent Sandpiper into a gallop, with Steve still in pursuit.

"Where are you going to sleep tonight?" he shouted.

"Go away and mind your own business," I shouted

back.

And I thought, if I stop at the bed and breakfast place, which Mr Brown suggested, Steve will pretend he's my father, guardian or uncle and tell everyone that I'm running away from home. And, because I'm just a teenager and he's past thirty they'll believe him, not me.

Children, I thought, are always at a disadvantage and grown-ups don't trust teenagers. In fact some grown-ups gang together to put us down. It's not fair.

Soon, hoping to leave Steve behind, I rode through deep bracken, where flies rose in black masses like locusts to torment us. Disheartened, I left them for softer terrain, with patches of water and tufts of coarse grass. Sandpiper sniffed the air and cantered with pricked ears and alert eyes, as though scenting danger. Then suddenly he took off, almost unseating me and covered about ten feet before touching ground again, while Tina ran in a wide arc, skirting the area. I looked back and saw Steve only a few yards behind me, his face grim, his cheeks reddened by wind and rain.

"Stop Carey, you..."

The last word was lost as his cycle dived into the bog, which Sandpiper, unknown to me, had jumped. Horrified I saw the dark spongy earth close over his head. Would he drown? He was my enemy, but I didn't want him dead, whatever his misdeeds.

"Steve!" I turned back but then I saw his head appear again, soaked in the peaty mixture which makes a bog what it is. He floundered for a moment then grabbed the stem of a small bush and pulled himself out. And stood, looking hopeless, helpless and aimless. And I thought: there is no way he can retrieve his cycle by himself, and I felt almost sorry for him, because I suspected he was really a wimp controlled by Hannah.

Then I rode on and on, trying to check my way on Mr Brown's map, which was too small-scale to show tracks across the moors, but convinced I was going in the right direction. And sleep came like a dark blanket and I almost fell from the saddle and then knew I could go no further. I looked at my animals and saw they were dead-tired too, and that settled the matter, Tina found a burn, where we all drank. I unrolled my sleeping bag, shared the chocolate Mrs Brown had put with the sandwiches with Tina, who also ate some of the pony nuts I fed to Sandpiper. Now I made a clumsy tether for him, out of his headcollar rope and reins, I found a strong stick, which I sharpened into a point with my penknife, before driving it into the ground as a tethering stake; an arrangement which would have failed any RSPCA inspection, but what could I do, when my eyes would barely focus and their lids felt lead-weighted? Then, like a dog, I dug myself a hollow, where I put my sleeping bag, and in moments all thoughts of Steve and Granny were blotted out by sleep.

When I wakened my world was moonlit, magical, touched everywhere with silver, and silent; no cars, no humans. I could have been on another planet. Too early, I thought, forcing myself to doze for another hour or so. Then, remembering my tablet, I dug again in my anorak pocket, found the bottle, unscrewed the top, fumbled, and let all the little white pills fall into the heather.

"Twit!"

In this unnerving silence my voice seemed loud and ugly, and Tina came to be with me.

"Sit, stay! Don't move!"

I found and swallowed one tablet and was about to collect the rest when Sandpiper strolled up looking important and, before I could stop him, trampled all the rest into the ground with his neat, black hoofs. Reins and rope do not readily knot together and he had broken loose from his tether, but this time he had stayed near, and that I told myself, fighting tears, was the lucky side of things.

I sat with my arms wrapped round my body and remembered how, before being prescribed the tablets, I had sometimes suffered two black-outs a day. Shaun had said stress was more of a trigger than the missing of a single pill, but, all the same, I decided I must find a doctor before the chemists shut.

Sandpiper had filled his belly on what grass he could find amongst the heather. Dogs can survive comfortably on one meal a day, but my tummy rumbled with hunger and I felt strangely detached from my surroundings. "I could easily faint," I told Tina, as I rolled up the sleeping bag and, not understanding a word, she wagged her tail and her eyes asked, "Any food?"

I had stopped at half past seven in the evening, and it was now five-thirty the next morning, and almost light. I stuffed the empty bottle into a pocket, tacked up Sandpiper and set off again, wondering what had happened to Steve and wishing I knew my way. If only there was someone to ask.

I was lost. An hour must have passed and an ache was starting in the back of my skull when I heard a shepherd whistling to his dog. Sandpiper's head came up. Tina pricked her ears. Filled with sudden hope, I stopped and let them search the landscape and, when Sandpiper's gaze settled, I followed it with my own eyes and saw a man in the valley below with a black and white collie, and sheep moving. "Hi, help," I shouted, and then Tina, who seemed to understand, led the way down a path, which would take us to those figures, who looked so wonderfully like farmyard toys.

CHAPTER EIGHTEEN

"You're up early," the handsome shepherd said.

"I'm heading south for Berwick or thereabouts," I replied.

"It's a fine pony you've got there and a bonnie dog," he told me. "Berwick's a fair way to go I'm thinking. Are you lost then?"

"Yes, and I need a telephone and a doctor."

"Och aye," the shepherd said, looking at my hair which I had combed with my fingers. "You'd best go to yonder farm." He pointed, "D'ye see it?"

I stared and stared in vain. "No."

He pointed again. "Have ye the short sight then?" he asked, turning round to watch his dog with the sheep. "Go back the way ye came, and follow the widest track," he continued a moment later. "Then ye would have to be blind not to see it. Fiona Macgregor's the name, a fine lass to be sure. Ye will not be wanting there."

I thanked the shepherd retraced out steps, leading Sandpiper in case he was tired. I took the wider track and soon saw a farm, hidden behind trees. I banged the heavy knocker on the wide oak door. Chains were undone and bolts drawn back and then I was face to face with Fiona Macgregor, a young fresh-faced woman only a few years older than me.

"I'm sorry to bother you," I began, feeling weak with hunger, "I was lost and the shepherd in the valley said you might let me use your phone."

"You've not slept out on the moors?" cried Fiona Macgregor.

"I was lost."

"You must be fair famished," she cried. "Here, we'll put the pony in the barn right away and you'll breakfast with me. I shall be right glad of your company, for it's awful lonely up here, with my man out all day and not a soul around."

While I settled Sandpiper, Fiona made porridge.

And I came back to a breakfast which would have set up even the hungriest and tallest person for the day.

"And there's a tin of cat food for the collie," Fiona said. "We don't farm the land," she explained. "That's done by my brother-in-law, Jamie. My husband works in the town. He leaves just after six of a morning and gets back at seven at night."

"That's sad for you," I said.

"You're right," cried Fiona, and for the next half hour she regaled me with all the problems in her life.

"You're not in love, are you?" she finished, staring at me with large blue eyes, "So maybe you'll not understand. But my Hamish is all the world to me, a gentle lovely man, and yet ...no, I won't say it, not even to a kind stranger like yourself."

"Perhaps you should get a job," I suggested, "In the town, too, then you could meet Hamish for lunch."

"No, no, he's with the lads in the pub midday," she said.

"You've not seen a red-bearded man with a motor-cycle?" I asked.

"No, we don't get that kind up here, too many bogs," she said. "Is he a relative then?"

"No, he pestered me."

"Och, that's terrible. Nobody's safe these days," said Fiona.

Eventually, after Fiona had told me the name of her doctor, I asked to use the phone, but once again there was no answer from Granny's number. Then I tactlessly offended Fiona by asking whether I could pay for my breakfast.

"As if I would take a penny from you. You've been a right tonic," she said.

And so, I thought, beautiful far away places are full of lonely women longing for travellers to break the tedium of their days. And riding on in the direction of Fiona's doctor, I was glad that, unlike Elspeth, Fiona had asked me little about my life and accepted the brief answers I gave her.

The doctor's house was white, with a timber fence to which I tied my animals, who were glad of a rest. The waiting room was empty and very soon the doctor, a gingery Scot with searching eyes, put his head round the door.

"Next please."

"Sit down, sit down," he said as I hovered in front of his desk. "Now what can I do for you young lady?"

I held out my empty tablet bottle, "I need more of these, please. I lost them on the moors."

He examined the details on the bottle. "And what do you take these for, may I ask?"

"Black-outs."

"What sort of black-outs."

Then I remembered Shaun's name for it. "Epilepsy," I said.

"You have fits."

"I suppose so," I replied.

"You must know," he insisted. "Are they fits or not? Petit mal or grand mal?"

I said nothing.

"Is that your pony and dog out there?" the doctor then asked, in an attempt to lighten the atmosphere.

"That's right. I'm on my way south - Duke of Edinburgh Award and a sponsored ride as well. It's great." I rushed on, glad to change the subject.

"And you slept out on the moor last night, no adders, I hope. I see a sprig of heather in your hair," he said.

"That's right, and somewhere along the way I lost my comb," I explained. "But these tablets ..." he turned the bottle over in his hand ... "It's not something we prescribe off the cuff so to speak. Carey Lovegrove," he mused, "not any relation of that media couple, are you?"

"Please lend me a pencil and paper," I pleaded. "And I'll write down the name and address of my specialist and also of my GP which I know by heart, and perhaps you could phone them, and then everything will be all right."

"A good idea, I can see you've got your head screwed on the right way," said the doctor, who now clearly thought I needed cheering up. He handed me a biro and prescription form.

"There you are," I said, the details written, glad that my handwriting is reasonably firm and clear. "Either can tell you all about me."

"It's best you wait outside while I speak to your GP," the doctor said, taking the paper. "Alison," he called to his nurse, "Can you give this young lady a comb, she's lost hers on the moors."

Twenty minutes later I left with the prescription in my pocket and the name of a chemist in the next small town. "Only a short ride today," I told my animals, "and we'll spend a night in a bed and breakfast place, and buy postcards to send to all the people who have helped us."

And I felt grown-up at last, a girl who could handle her own affairs. Yet, in my heart, I knew that without Tina and Sandpiper I would have given up long ago. It wasn't just the fact that I needed a pony to carry me, it was their company which kept me from despair. All my life I had needed someone to talk to and if you talk to yourself people think you're mad, whereas if you talk to your pony or dog, you are only thought quaint.

CHAPTER NINETEEN

The rest of that day was magic. Small, frilled clouds chased each other across a blue sky; the sun came and went; a gentle breeze broke up the stillness of the summer air, so we were never too hot. When we came to a more built-up area we found side roads with wide soft verges on which to trot.

Fiona's breakfast kept hunger at bay until tea-time, even though we rested for an hour under trees - a sure recipe for hunger - and I reckoned that by four o'clock we had covered thirty miles. But now water became a problem, for we had left the moors and burns behind.

Even then our luck was in, for when I knocked on a door and asked for a drink for us all, it was opened by a small lively woman, with shining brown eyes, who cried out with joy at seeing us.

"What a wonderful trio! Of course, a bucket for your gorgeous pony, a bowl for the dog and a glass for you."

As we all drank, she said, "What a lovely visitation!" When I told her where we were going she announced she was full of admiration for my venture.

"So few people have pluck these days," she declared. "And where are you spending the night?"

"Under the stars." I pointed to my sleeping bag. "It's waterproof."

"Beautiful dreamer, wake unto me, Starlight and dewdrop are waiting for thee..." quoted the lively little woman. "Why not under the stars in my orchard?"

"But," I began.

"She floats she hesitates; in a word, she's a woman."

"You have a quotation for everything," I said.

"Racine. But women are not like that now, are they? Make up your mind. *Procrastination is the thief of time.*"

"I would love to sleep in your orchard. Thank you very much," I replied, "but Sandpiper might eat all your apples."

"No, it's a cherry orchard - *loveliest of trees, the cherry now* - Housman, a splendid if gloomy poet. Listen ...?"

"Carey."

"Listen Carey. I've even got a verandah you can borrow if it rains."

"Thanks a million. You are so kind."

"No, it's my pleasure, Carey," she insisted. "I'm Annette Younger, by the way, retired English teacher, and you're going to earn your keep by telling me all about your school. I'm writing a novel, you see, and I'm terribly out of date. Now follow me."

"After we had settled Sandpiper in an overgrown cherry orchard we went indoors and drank tea, ate buttered buns and talked, until my eyes closed.

Annette Younger gave me supper and opened a tin

of Irish stew, which Tina wolfed down with a slice of wholemeal bread. And I slept, as I had hoped, under a wide and starry sky and wakened when Sandpiper sniffed my hair.

"It's been marvellous having you," Annette Younger declared over breakfast. "Everything is grist to a writer's mill. And the debt is all mine, because you've given me a splendid idea for a story about a convent school girl."

So I left with a clear conscience; yet, in a strange way Annette's cheerfulness made me feel lonely and quite suddenly I was sick and tired of my journey.

It started to rain again, but early in the afternoon I found a bed and breakfast bungalow, which took dogs, and the owner's son, a farmer, provided a field for Sandpiper. That night I slept twelve hours without a break.

When I paid the bill next morning I had only a few pounds left so I decided that, whatever the weather, I should have to sleep out. Then sadly I would try to sell my saddle, which had been a present from Mum, and continue my ride bareback.

And where was Steve? And why had the police stopped looking for me? As I trudged on, leading Sandpiper to rest his back, these were only two of the questions which plagued me.

CHAPTER TWENTY

When you have money you are somebody; when you
have none you are nothing. When you have money
grown-ups treat you as an equal. You say, I will take
this room for the night or I will not. And they wait for
your words. You make decisions; you have power of a
sort. These thoughts crossed my mind the next day,
as I set out on a full stomach but with only a few
pounds left. Then I remembered seeing a homeless
girl about my age in London. She had asked me for
money and I had said, "No, go away." She had shown
me a baby's bottle and spoken of a "little boy," and I
had refused to believe her. I supposed now that this
girl had run away like me, because her home had become a place of fear. I guessed she had told lies as I
told lies to live from day to day - or she may have had
a baby, because, after all, I was old enough to have a
baby, too. That girl, her hair tangled like mine, her
face paper-white, probably had nothing, while I had
a pony, a dog and well-off parents who would return
and rescue me in a few weeks' time. And, I hoped, a

grandmother too, who would make me a cup of coffee and say, "Now sit down, darling, and let's talk it through."

Of course, I thought, that girl could be on drugs, a truant from school, a criminal, but from now on I would dig in my pocket and give begging girls any money I had.

It was a sweltering day. Tina panted and Sandpiper sweated and cats sat in doorways waiting to be let in, and the fume-laden air made me cough. When I decided to ride to Granny's I had thought of quiet roads, picnics in the sun, moorland and cool glades, forgetting that if you must move quickly from A to B you may be forced to take busy thoroughfares. Now even the roads which had seemed unimportant on Mr Brown's map turned out to be popular with caravaners, motorists and, occasionally, huge trucks whose drivers were perhaps, like me, avoiding the motorways.

For five miles I rode and then, as the traffic increased after ten o'clock, I walked leading Sandpiper by his reins and Tina on his headcollar rope.

By lunchtime I was exhausted with trying to keep my animals in when great hissing lorries belted by. There was no escape and for the first time, I felt like giving up.

I saw an open gate. In despair I led my animals into a stony field. I unbridled Sandpiper, put on his headcollar and lay in the grass with Tina beside me. I slept, dreaming that Mum and Dad were back and Steve was kneeling at Dad's feet asking for forgiveness, dreamed, until suddenly the rope was snatched from my hand, as Sandpiper broke loose and trotted towards the road.

"Stop! Whoa! Walk!"

I leapt to my feet, turned my ankle over and fell, ripping my jeans and tearing my hands and knees on stones.

"Sandpiper!"

I saw it all, the wheels of a great lorry hitting him; his toppling body, his flanks crushed, his head...

Then Tina, with a collie's instinct to round-up straying animals, raced ahead of Sandpiper and, nipping first at his muzzle and then his heels, turned him and brought him back.

"Oh Tina. Tina!" I kissed and patted her, then inspected my bloody knees and hands, which she tried to lick, and my tattered jeans - but grunge was still in then, so who cared?

Five minutes later we were back on that terrible road, only this time I limped as I led my animals. Soon we came to a steep hill, where my blistered feet started to hurt for the first time, and Sandpiper took fright at a plastic bag, fluttering in a hedge. Snorting, he swung his quarters out and a fast car missed him by inches. Then Tina's nerves shattered and as he pulled back she rushed forward, so I felt torn in two. Behind us a large truck changed gear as it climbed the hill - a vehicle, I thought, big enough to pulp us all - and I couldn't put an arm out to slow it down, because mine were both needed to control my animals. I expected the driver to hoot his horn, but instead he breaked gently and shouted, "Having trouble?" And I yelled, "Yes." And moments later he had parked his truck and taken Sandpiper's reins.

"Want to get killed?" he asked. "Are you plain daft or what?"

"I'm trying to reach Yorkshire," I replied.

"Yorkshire - on these roads? Look," he pointed. "See that farm drive - up there. Run!" He led Sandpiper and I followed with Tina.

"Right, wait, while I bring the truck up. Does he load all right?"

"Yes, yes, I think so."

And only then did I realise my rescuer was driving a cattle truck.

"I'd best take the three of you home," he said.

CHAPTER TWENTY ONE

I was taking a risk, accepting a lift from a stranger, but his name - CHAS COLES HORSE AND CATTLE TRANSPORTER, was on the side of his truck. He had snapshots of his wife and two daughters stuck on the dashboard. He told me had taken six shetland ponies from a stud in England to a new breeder in Scotland.

"Back to where they belong," he joked.

"Not all the way to the Shetland Isles?"

"No not quite as far as that," he said. "Where have you come from then?"

There is something relaxing about sitting high in the cab of a large truck, looking down on small vehicles and with Tina beside me I felt safe. Yet I hesitated, because I was sick of lying and guessed Chas Coles would know that sponsored riders and contestants for the Duke of Edinburgh Award don't take lifts in trucks. Nor are they expected to travel on busy roads.

"Not running away from home, are you?" he now asked, glancing at me with deep-set blue eyes, in a deeply lined face which looked as though he never slept.

"Yes."

"You're joking."

"My parents are away. They left me miles from anywhere in their summer cottage to be looked after by a
horrible half-sister, who hates me, because Dad left
her mother for mine. She's supposed to have grown
up in Australia, but she doesn't speak with an Australian accent and she has a horrible friend called
Steve, whom I loathe, a right creep, and so I decided
to run away to Granny's."

"Not all Australians speak like the kids in *Neighbours*," observed Charles Coles. "And where is this
Granny of yours."

"Didn't I tell you? - Yorkshire." I named the village.

"Not so far away then, you've nearly made it," he
said. "But it beats me why you didn't go by coach or
train. You could have left the pony behind."

"I want Sandpiper at Granny's," I said, slowly, as I
tried to sort out for the first time my exact motives.
"We only go to the cottage in the summer, whereas I
go to Granny for all my half-terms and usually for
three weeks at Easter, and there's a riding school
nearby and people to ride with, and a pony club, and
I've got a friend called Kirsty, and Tina likes it there,
too." Suddenly I wanted to talk until my tongue was
too tired to utter another word, but it seemed wrong
to tell a stranger what I had meant to tell Granny.

An hour later Charles Coles pulled off the road. "Fish
and chips?" he asked, "Before we cross the border."

"Great," I said. "Please can you get a double helping

of chips? - Tina loves them." I opened my purse.

"I don't want any money," he said. "Lemonade - all right? And water for the pony?"

He fetched a bucket from the back of the truck, where, Sandpiper, who was bedded down in straw, with an armful of hay to eat, moved about restlessly.

"He'll be all right when we get moving again," Mr Coles told me ..."Here," he dug in a first aid kit, "ointment to put on your knees and hands."

"Where exactly are you going?" I asked when we had eaten and were on the road again, and about to cross into England. He named a village I had never heard of.

"Not too far," but I'm running a bit late. I've got some cattle to pick up and drive down to a farm twenty miles further on. I'll drop you off a couple of miles from your Granny's - all right? I'd like to take you to her door, but ..."

"Oh please don't worry."

"Can't help worrying when you've got daughters of your own like," he said. "I'd kill mine if I heard they had taken a lift from a man they didn't know, but then they wouldn't be out with a pony and dog on a busy road anyway. You must have driven up with your Mum and Dad, you must have known what the roads were like."

"We flew."

"Flew -Did they charter a plane or something?"

"No, no - to the nearest town and then by mini-cab to the ferry."

"Wealthy people then - your Mum and Dad?"

"They earn every penny themselves," I said, uncomfortably because I hate feeling privileged. "They work all hours."

"So there's no time left for you," suggested Charles Coles, as we crossed the border. "There's a price to pay for everything."

"They're fine," I sighed. "England! It's brilliant to be back, although I do love Scotland, and everybody there was so sweet."

Then my eyes closed and I slept, until Tina's barks and the sound of the truck's ramp dropping woke me. A village green was bathed in pale evening sunlight. The surrounding stone cottages, their gardens bright with roses, honeysuckle and hollyhocks and, at the back, neat rows of vegetables, were familiar. Ducks swam, as always on the pond.

"I know where I am," I cried. And Tina, who knew too, wagged her tail. "I used to ride here with the school."

"Whoa, steady there. Do you want the sleeping bag strapped on again?" asked Mr Coles, as he led Sandpiper down the ramp. "Not too far to your Nan's, is it?"

"No. Brilliant, thanks a thousand." I tried to memorise his address, painted in small letters close to the cab's door. "I shall send you a postcard of Granny's village, so you know I arrived. Now please how much do I owe you?"

"Nothing, nothing at all."

"But I .. Mum and Dad...."

"Well, I must get going," he said.

"But I think you saved my life," I cried.

"Maybe I did, maybe I didn't," he replied. "We can't always sort out the ifs and buts in life, can we? Now listen, Carey - you did say your'name was Carey, didn't you? - don't do that sort of thing again, because it causes a lot of worry to a lot of people." He bridled Sandpiper and tied on the sleeping bag.

"No, I won't," I said, feeling terribly humbled.

"Here you are," he handed me the reins. "Take care and watch how you go. Ta-ta and all the best." He jumped into his cab, started the engine and that was the last I ever saw of him.

CHAPTER TWENTY TWO

Tina, who knew the way, walked with her lovely black white-tipped tail raised, her head high. The journey had strengthened her muscles. She looked superb. Sandpiper sniffed the air and lengthened his stride, because he, too, sensed I was no longer worried. His coat had grown browner, like day lilies, his mane shone tar-black in the late afternoon sunshine. Now I was seeing them both through Granny's eyes, for she had once been an expert horsewoman and dog owner and I valued her opinion.

Would she say, "My goodness Carey, you've looked after your animals well," confirming I was responsible, had overcome my disability and needed no allowances made for me.

We came to another Green - Granny's Green - shaded by great beech trees; its grass, after the wet summer, verdant as peridots. Its squat church caught in a long shaft of sunlight; its pond alive, too, with ducks, and the black chains that marked its boundaries newly painted.

A few old people sat on seats given in memory of the

dead. Dead ... Granny dead? No; she was too young, too lively, too committed to life. And, besides, it was hard to fear the worst when the sky was so wonderfully blue; the air fresh from the hills and my ride almost over. What would she say when I walked through her garden gate? I forgot my sore hands and aching knees, my torn jeans and untidy hair, for in my mind I now saw not me, but her, small and indomitable.

I reached her cottage; the apple trees in the front garden were laden with fruit; purple plums were ripening, and the roses she had trained to climb the trunks were in flower.

"Granny, it's me - Carey," I stood in the porch banging the heavy knocker and ringing the bell in turn, while Sandpiper yanked at the reins and Tina ran round the back. Then I saw Granny's tabby cat purring inside the kitchen - "Patsy, Patsy, where's Granny?"

I hitched Sandpiper to the gate, went round the back and found the spare key Granny kept under a flower pot and went inside. A tray was laid with a plate, cup and saucer, cutlery, a toastrack and a pot of honey, as if for tea - or was it breakfast? How long had it waited there unused?

I was wandering round the cottage when I heard Sandpiper pull back and break his reins. I ran outside and I found him eating a valuable shrub.

"Wicked."

I led Sandpiper to the back and locked up the cottage. Then, leaving Tina inside, I took him to the riding school and persuaded its owner, Lucy Gatte, to keep him for the night.

"Have you seen Granny lately?" I asked.

"Mrs Mancroft? - No, as a matter of fact I haven't," she said. "I like him," she added, watching Sandpiper walk away across the field, "a true dun, tougher than the palominos everyone wants these days. Are you all right, Carey? You don't look your usual, cheerful self. And your knees ..."

"Absolutely, but it was a long truck ride," I replied, reluctant to waste time telling Lucy about my journey.

I returned to the cottage, made myself tea, found and ate a packet of biscuits, gave Tina a tin of Patsy's meat, took a hot bath - the gas heater still worked - and changed into a cotton dress I had left with Granny. Then the telephone rang and an Australian voice said, "Mrs Mancroft? Long time no see, it's Hannah."

"Hannah..." I said, my heart pounding. "You sound different."

"Who am I speaking to?"

"Oh, don't be a twit." I said, keeping cool. "You know who I am - Carey. What are you playing at now?"

"Carey Lovegrove, pleased to meet you. I'm your half sister Hannah."

"Hannah's in Scotland," I said.

"No, that was cancelled. Don't you remember? Such a shame. It would have been real good getting to know each other there."

"But I have been there with someone called Hannah," I told her.

"I guess we're getting our lines crossed," this other Hannah said. "Your father faxed me at work and cancelled the arrangement."

"I think we've got to talk," I said. "Where are you?"

"York. I've come to see your mother, Carey."

"Mum's somewhere in the Caucasus. She couldn't get in touch because Hannah forgot her mobile phone."

"Your mother's in hospital, here in York."

"I think I'm going crazy," I said.

"I've actually come from London on the coach to see her. I heard she was very seriously ill. I thought it might be my only chance."

"No one told me. I've been on the island with someone who called herself Hannah."

"An imposter!"

It was too much. "I want Granny," I said and burst into tears, which was, of course, a very babyish thing to do.

"Honey, I'm sorry, but there's been some dirty work going on."

"The fax was a fake," I said, trying to collect my wits and think straight. "Hannah, the fake Hannah came to the island to smuggle."

"Listen Carey, I think I must go to the hospital right now and we must talk later. Let me give you my number at the hotel so Mrs Mancroft can call me there later."

"Right." I reached for the pen and pad Granny always keeps by her phone. "Go ahead."

I wrote it down and then, feeling bemused, I asked if this Australian Hannah could give me the name

119

and number of the hospital where Mum was, and she did.

And then Granny walked in, looking older and very tired.

CHAPTER TWENTY THREE

"Your mother was taken ill a day after she left," Granny said, "and no one seemed to know what it was, so she flew home. At first she was in hospital in London and I stayed there and then, when she was much better, she managed to get herself transferred to York to be near me. Of course, she wouldn't let Cosmo come back with her, because of the book. And she didn't want you to know, because she was afraid you would be upset. Then, when she did try to phone herself, she couldn't get through. Now I know why."

It was next morning. We were eating breakfast at a round table in the kitchen. The night before we had talked mostly about my problems on the island, but both of us had found it so hard to stay awake that, after eating an omelette and some ice cream, we went to bed. "No one has yet identified the virus which attacked her," Granny added. She was two days in intensive care. Look, here's the detective inspector. That's quick work. I only phoned an hour ago."

He wasn't like Taggart or Morse or any other TV detective I had seen. He was young and blue-eyed and very charming, and I told him absolutely everything I could remember about Hannah and her friends. And he told me that there was an illegal trade in coral from the Philippines, and one of the easiest ways to smuggle anything like that was in boats, landing on small beaches at night, where you can avoid customs. "They probably kept it for a time in that old oak chest," he said.

He left at eleven o'clock after drinking a mug of coffee, and we heard no more for a week, and then we saw in a newspaper that fledgling golden eagles had been found, ready for transit in a remote Scottish island - our island - and the couple at the Wildlife Centre had been arrested.

But before then, Mum had come home, and the real Hannah had walked through the door, looking very like Cosmo - flaxen and tall and open-faced, the sort of girl I wished I was. When I described the other Hannah, she said, "Oh, that's cracked it - Debbie, for heaven's sake, the girl I met in hospital, a temp, filling in for someone else. She needed accommodation and my apartment was too big, so it seemed to make sense ..Oh sure thing that was a mistake, and I told her all about myself, and how I wanted to meet my real father, whom I hadn't seen since I was two, and about the island and you, and she was real sympathetic."

"So she sent a fax?"

"Who else! It was an embarrassment coming to hospital like that, no kidding."

"It's weird to think she combined coral smuggling with eagles," I said.

"I guess the eagles were Steve's brainwave, don't you?" Hannah said.

"The Mafia are looking for new opportunities all the time," Mum remarked. "They have their fingers in every pie in every country."

"You mean there was a Mr Big behind Hannah and Steve?" I asked incredulously. "They seemed so inefficient."

"Lots of criminals are," Mum said.

Then we turned to my future.

"I can't go back to boarding school, not now. I feel too old," I said. "And I can handle my trouble myself."

"A London day school?" Mum put an arm round me.

"But you're always away," I complained. "The flat gets spooky; Tina's tired of pavements. And everybody knows I'm your daughter, which makes them think I'm spoilt and stuck-up. It's difficult, Mum, honestly ... you've no idea!"

"She could stay here and go to the local comprehensive and maybe call herself Mancroft, if the headteacher agrees," Granny suggested, "And perhaps on to the sixth form college."

"And arrange a share for Sandpiper at Lucy's place, until I'm too big for him." I added, for I was already half-way to arranging that with a girl called Jane. "I want to teach him to jump."

"We would insist on paying for Carey's keep, of course," said Mum.

"I like cooking so I'd help out, and Tina and Patsy

have made friends," I added.

"It would be company," Granny said. "And you could pick the apples I can't reach and clean the gutters for me. I'd really love to have you here, Carey. And, by the way, Melanie, I've got myself a little job at the teashop."

"Brilliant," I cried. "And I'm good on ladders."

"It sounds a great idea." Hannah switched on the kettle. "More tea anyone?"

Later when Mum was in bed and I was sitting at her side, I asked a question which had been troubling me ever since I met the fake Hannah.

"What happens when I have an attack?"

"Your brain cuts off, that's all," Mum said.

"No, how do I look?"

"Oh look - well blank."

"I fall, don't I?"

"Yes you fall," Mum said, " and then you lie still."

"Don't I twitch?"

"A bit."

"Do I, do I foam at the mouth?" I asked, " Or anything else."

"Oh no," Mum said, "you just lie for a bit and then get up as though nothing had happened. That's all."

"Promise?"

"Promise."

But I couldn't be sure Mum was telling the truth, because I knew she wouldn't want me to know the worst.

"Anyway," she added, taking my hand, "You won't have any more attacks, so long as you take your medicine, and by the time you're eighteen it will have died down a bit."

"I know it's something I must learn to live with," I replied. "And in a way it's not as handicapping as asthma. I met a boy called Shaun who said ..."

Then the telephone rang, and it was Dad. "Carey! I didn't expect you to answer," he exclaimed.

"Life's been quite crazy, Hannah wasn't Hannah ..."

I tried to tell him all that had happened, and gabbled so much, he became confused and asked to speak to Mum.

"How does she look?" he asked.

"Pale and thin, but great."

"The press haven't been on to her?"

"No," I said remembering with pride mixed with regret, that Mum was famous.

"Good," Dad said. "Try to keep it that way. Now, where is she?"

They talked for ages, for Dad was now in Moscow, so telephoning was easy, and although I left the room, I heard my name mentioned from time to time.

"Your Dad agrees," Mum called. "You can stay with Granny, but please write him a letter, explaining in great detail *exactly* what happened. It can go care of the British Embassy."

"The book?" I asked.

"Great, everything's great. He's met all the right people." Mum told me. "Darling, are you absolutely sure you'll be happy here?"

"Oh yes, it's what I want," I said.

And that's how it was. I wrote to everyone who had

helped me and two days later Steve, who had returned to the island, and the fake Hannah were caught, while Mercy and her accomplice escaped. Later Shaun came to stay. And I appeared in court, but that's another story.